THE HIGHER ANIMALS:

A Mark Twain Bestiary

THE HIGHER ANIMALS:

A Mark Twain Bestiary
Edited by Maxwell Geismar
Drawings by Jean-Claude Suarès

THOMAS Y. CROWELL COMPANY NEW YORK
ESTABLISHED 1834

Designed by Steve Heller

Library of Congress Cataloging in Publication Data

Clemens, Samuel Langhorne, 1835-1910.
    The higher animals.
    1. Animals, Legends and stories of.   I. Geismar, Maxwell David, 1909-   II. Title.
PS1303.G38   1976   818′. 4′07   76-6563
ISBN 0-690-01149-0

Manufactured in the United States of America

2 3 4 5 6 7 8 9 10

Thanks are due to Harper & Row, Publishers, Inc., for permission to quote the following copyright material.

From *Mark Twain: Letters from the Earth*, edited by Bernard DeVoto: pages 223-224, "The Earl and the Anaconda;" 80-81, "Eve Milks a Cow," from "Eve's Autobiography," copyright © 1962 by the Mark Twain Company "A Cat-Tale," copyright © 1959, by The Mark Twain Company.

From *The Mysterious Stranger and Other Stories* by Mark Twain: "A Fable," copyright 1909 by Harper and Brothers.

From *Mark Twain's Autobiography*, Volume I, edited by Albert Bigelow Paine: 227, "On Venetian Flies;" 103-104, "Snakes, Bats and Aunt Patsy," copyright 1935 by Clara Gabrilowitsch.

From *Mark Twain's Notebook*, edited by Albert Bigelow Paine: 35-36, "Seagoing Rats;" 234, "The Hoot Owl;" 248, "A Letter to Kipling, August 16, 1895," copyright 1935 by the Mark Twain Company.

From *Mark Twain in Eruption*, edited by Bernard DeVoto: 22-24, "On Naturalists;" 221-222, "Uncle Lem's Composite Dog," copyright 1922 by Harper & Brothers.

By permission of Harper & Row, Publishers, Inc.

Dedicated to
That Noble Soul, Hankins Geismar

BOOKS BY MAXWELL GEISMAR

THE NOVEL IN AMERICA

Writers in Crisis: The American Novel, 1925-1940
(*Studies of Ring Lardner, Ernest Hemingway, John Dos Passos,*
William Faulkner, Thomas Wolfe, John Steinbeck)
The Last of the Provincials: The American Novel, 1915-1925
(*Studies of H.L. Mencken, Sinclair Lewis, Willa Cather,*
Sherwood Anderson, F. Scott Fitzgerald)
Rebels and Ancestors: The American Novel, 1890-1915
(*Studies of Frank Norris, Stephen Crane, Jack London,*
Ellen Glasgow, Theodore Dreiser)
American Moderns: From Rebellion to Conformity
Henry James and the Jacobites
Mark Twain: An American Prophet
Ring Lardner and the Portrait of Folly

EDITOR

The Ring Lardner Reader
The Walt Whitman Reader
The Portable Thomas Wolfe
Sherwood Anderson: Short Stories
Jack London: Short Stories
Mark Twain and the Three R's
The Higher Animals: A Mark Twain Bestiary

INTRODUCTION

What is the point of an introduction to a Mark Twain Bestiary? None at all, that I can see, except to move the reader as fast as possible from this page to the Twainian text proper, with the handsome illustrations by Jean-Claude Suarès.

Can any introduction explain or analyze the real quality of Mark Twain's prose?—which is always at its peak, it seems to me, in the descriptions of the animals he has met and known. Twain wrote about animals as though he was one, but the enigma, the fascination of his animal studies, profiles, and portraits is a little more complex than that. Along with Walt Whitman, Twain is one of the two great primitive poets in the American language; and his poetry was never more clearly expressed than in the heroes, villains, dupes, and clowns of the animal world.

They are marvelously entertaining; but they are *themselves* always, too. Mark Twain was one of those artists who saw reality true. There was nothing that ever came between that bold, impudent, unwavering, insistent *stare* of his—that painter's eye, that journalistic nose for sniffing out the real nature of things, that remarkably rich, fresh, open and encyclopedic mind of his—and the world he lived in.

The world he lived in; the world around him; the real world of hard, objective materiality which is *there*. In Twain there is none of that literary "ambiguity," so fashionable today, in which the writer's "fancy," or his imaginative rendering of things, takes precedence over the factuality of his subject—until we hardly know which is the writer's fancy, which is the subject he is describing. No, there is a world outside; and there is Mark Twain surveying it; and the fusion, at its best, is genius.

Twain would never falsify any detail of his animal subjects (except, obviously, in his tall tales) for a literary effect or a purely human prejudice. These are animal animals to their core; and that is maybe one reason they are such a relief from the human animals we think we are more familiar with. From the beginning to the end of his long career Mark Twain not only lived in this animal kingdom but he also rejoiced in it—he celebrated it. While his view of mankind may have changed with the tragic wisdom of age, his pleasure in his animal friends remained constant.

From the Jumping Frog of 1867, from the melancholy mares and disdainful, haughty camels of *The Innocents Abroad* in 1869, from the hound pups, coyotes, jackass-rabbits and Mexican Plugs of *Roughing It* in 1872, to the dachshunds and Delhi monkeys, Indian crows, phosphorescent porpoises and Australian magpies of *Following the Equator* in 1897. Yes, to the Equator book and beyond it: to Twain's final volumes of letters, notebooks and autobiography in the 1900s—this great artist and culture hero lived continually, deeply, richly in that animal kingdom which he created with such affection and humor, pleasure and delight, with such an abundance of innocence and such an absence of egotism; that Twainian animal kingdom so faithful to reality and so unmistakably his own.

And even beyond this it extended; beyond the limits of his lifetime. The last of these extraordinary animal personae come from such posthumous and contemporary Twain publications as *The Mysterious Stranger and Other Tales* in 1922; from Bernard DeVoto's *Mark Twain in Eruption* in 1940, and the same editor's *Letters from the Earth* in 1962. Part of Mark Twain's extraordinary presence in American literature as a whole derives from the fact that almost as many books by him have been published since his death as before it. He is a writer "who speaks from the grave," as he said about himself, and therefore tells us the truth. He is a writer whose spirit continues to live with us, to haunt us and influence us, to chastise us perhaps, and remind us of an America which is past, which in his person was bolder and better than we dare to be, more humane and generous and aspiring and free in spirit.

But what would the members of Twain's animal kingdom have to say about such matters? To them there was not much use in reflecting on pasts and futures; to them there was only the immediate present, rewarding or fearful. Still casting about in my own mind for the reasons why this book was so different in the making from other books, I think that may be it. Everything in these pages lives completely and fully, sharply and deeply, in the eternal light of the present; there is no past, no future here, except as a faint shadow from our transient human existence. That is why Mark Twain's animal kingdom will live forever; or at least until, as he knew, man decides otherwise.

—Maxwell Geismar

Harrison, New York
May 1, 1976

There are no wild animals till man makes them so.

I have been studying the traits and dispositions of the "lower animals" (so-called), and contrasting them with the traits and dispositions of man. I find the result humiliating to me. For it obliges me to renounce my allegiance to the Darwinian theory of the Ascent of Man from the Lower Animals; since it now seems plain to me that the theory ought to be vacated in favor of a new and truer one, this new and truer one to be named the Descent of Man from the Higher Animals.

A

ALLIGATORS

Unfortunate tourists! People humbugged them with stupid and silly lies, and then laughed at them for believing and printing the same. They told Mrs. Trollope that the alligators—or crocodiles, as she calls them—were terrible creatures; and backed up the statement with a blood-curdling account of how one of these slandered reptiles crept into a squatter cabin one night, and ate up a woman and five children. The woman, by herself, would have satisfied any ordinarily impossible alligator; but no, these liars must make him gorge the five children besides.

THE ANT

Now and then, while we rested, we watched the laborious ant at his work. I found nothing new in him—certainly nothing to change my opinion of him. It seems to me that in the matter of intellect the ant must be a strangely overrated bird. During many summers, now, I have watched him, when I ought to have been in better business, and I have not yet come across a living ant that seemed to have any more sense than a dead one. I refer to the ordinary ant, of course; I have had no experience of those wonderful Swiss and African ones which vote, keep drilled armies, hold slaves, and dispute about religion. Those particular ants may be all that the naturalist paints them, but I am persuaded that the average ant is a sham. I admit his industry, of course; he is the hardest-working creature in the world—when anybody is looking—but his leather-headedness is the point I make against him. He goes out foraging, he makes a capture, and then what does he do? Go home? No—he goes anywhere but home. He doesn't know where home is. His home may be only three feet away—no matter, he can't find it. He makes his capture as I have said; it is generally something which can be of no sort of use to himself or anybody else; it is usually seven times bigger than it ought to be; he hunts out the awkwardest place to take hold of it; he lifts it bodily up in the air by main force, and starts; not toward home, but in the opposite direction; not calmly and wisely, but with a frantic haste which is wasteful of his strength; he fetches up against a pebble, and instead of going around it, he climbs over it backward dragging his booty after him, tumbles down on the other side, jumps up in a passion, kicks the dust off his clothes, moistens his hands, grabs his property viciously, yanks it this way, then that, shoves it ahead of him a moment, turns tail and lugs it after him another moment, gets madder and madder, then presently hoists it into the air and goes tearing away in an entirely new direction; comes to a weed; it never occurs to him to go around it; no, he must climb it; and he does climb it, dragging his worthless property to the top—which is as bright a thing to do as it would be for me to carry a sack of flour from Heidelberg to Paris by way of Strasburg steeple; when he gets up there he finds that that is not the place; takes a cursory glance at the scenery and either climbs down again or tumbles down, and starts off once more—as usual, in a new direction. At the end of half an hour, he fetches up within six inches of the place he started from and lays his burden down; meantime he has been over all the ground for two yards around, and climbed all the weeds and pebbles he came across. Now he wipes the sweat from his brow, strokes his limbs, and then marches aimlessly off, in as violent a hurry as ever. He traverses a good deal of zigzag country, and by and by stumbles on his same booty again. He does not remember to have ever seen it before; he looks around to see which is not the way home, grabs his bundle and starts; he goes through the same adventures he had before; finally stops to rest, and a friend comes along. Evidently the friend remarks that a last year's grasshopper leg is a very noble acquisition, and inquires where he got it. Evidently the proprietor does not remember exactly where he did get it, but thinks he got it "around here somewhere." Evidently the friend contracts to help him freight it home. Then, with a judgment peculiarly antic (pun not intentional), they take hold of opposite ends of that grasshopper leg and begin to tug with all their might in opposite directions. Presently they take a rest and confer together. They decide that something is wrong, they can't make out what. Then they go at it again, just as before. Same result. Mutual recriminations follow. Evidently each accuses the other of being an obstructionist. They warm up, and the dispute ends in a fight. They lock themselves together and chew each other's jaws for a while; then they roll and tumble on the ground till one loses a horn or a leg and has to haul off for repairs. They make up and go to work again in the same old insane way, but the crippled ant is at a disadvantage; tug as he may, the other one drags off the booty and him at the end of it. Instead of giving up, he hangs on, and gets his shins bruised against every ob-

struction that comes in the way. By and by, when that grasshopper leg has been dragged all over the same old ground once more, it is finally dumped at about the spot where it originally lay, the two perspiring ants inspect it thoughtfully and decide that dried grasshopper legs are a poor sort of property after all, and then each starts off in a different direction to see if he can't find an old nail or something else that is heavy enough to afford entertainment and at the same time valueless enough to make an ant want to own it.

There in the Black Forest, on the mountainside, I saw an ant go through with such a performance as this with a dead spider of fully ten times his own weight. The spider was not quite dead, but too far gone to resist. He had a round body the size of a pea. The little ant—observing that I was noticing—turned him on his back, sunk his fangs into his throat, lifted him into the air and started vigorously off with him, stumbling over little pebbles, stepping on the spider's legs and tripping himself up, dragging him backward, shoving him bodily ahead, dragging him up stones six inches high instead of going around them, climbing weeds twenty times his own height and jumping from their summits—and finally leaving him in the middle of the road to be confiscated by any other fool of an ant that wanted him. I measured the ground which this ass traversed, and arrived at the conclusion that what he had accomplished inside of twenty minutes would constitute some such job as this—relatively speaking—for a man; to wit: to strap two eight-hundred-pound horses together, carry them eighteen hundred feet, mainly over (not around) boulders averaging six feet high, and in the course of the journey climb up and jump from the top of one precipice like Niagara, and three steeples, each a hundred and twenty feet high; and then put the horses down, in an exposed place, without anybody to watch them, and go off to indulge in some other idiotic miracle for vanity's sake.

Science has recently discovered that the ant does not lay up anything for winter use. This will knock him out of literature, to some extent. He does not work, except when people are looking, and only then when the observer has a green, naturalistic look, and seems to be taking notes. This amounts to deception, and will injure him for the Sunday-schools. He has not judgment enough to know what is good to eat from what isn't. This amounts to ignorance, and will impair the world's respect for him. He cannot stroll around a stump and find his way home again. This amounts to idiocy, and once the damaging fact is established, thoughtful people will cease to look up to him, the sentimental will cease to fondle him. His vaunted industry is but a vanity and of no effect, since he never gets home with anything he starts with. This disposes of the last remnant of his reputation and wholly destroys his main usefulness as a moral agent, since it will make the sluggard hesitate to go to him any more. It is strange, beyond comprehension, that so manifest a humbug as the ant has been able to fool so many nations and keep it up so many ages without being found out.

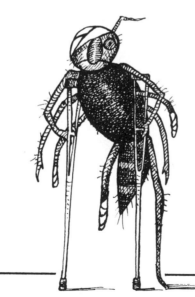

THE ASS

There is no character, howsoever good and fine, but it can be destroyed by ridicule, howsoever poor and witless. Observe the ass, for instance: his character is about perfect, he is the choicest spirit among all the humbler animals, yet see what ridicule has brought him to. Instead of feeling complimented when we are called an ass, we are left in doubt.

THE AUSTRALIAN MAGPIE

On the way we saw the usual birds—the beautiful little green parrots, the magpie, and some others; and also the slender native bird of modest plumage and the eternally forgettable name—the bird that is the smartest among birds, and can give a parrot thirty to one in the game and then talk him to death. I cannot recall the bird's name. I think it begins with M. I wish it began with G, or something that a person can remember.

The magpie was out in great force, in the fields and on the fences. He is a handsome large creature, with snowy white decorations, and is a singer; he has a murmurous

rich note that is lovely. He was once modest, even diffident; but he lost all that when he found out that he was Australia's sole musical bird. He has talent, and cuteness, and impudence; and in his tame state he is a most satisfactory pet—never coming when he is called, always coming when he isn't, and studying disobedience as an accomplishment. He is not confined, but loafs all over the house and grounds, like the laughing jackass. I think he learns to talk, I know he learns to sing tunes, and his friends say that he knows how to steal without learning. I was acquainted with a tame magpie in Melbourne. He had lived in a lady's house several years, and believed he owned it. The lady had tamed him, and in return he had tamed the lady. He was always on deck when not wanted, always having his own way, always tyrannizing over the dog, and always making the cat's life a slow sorrow and a martyrdom. He knew a number of tunes and could sing them in perfect time and tune; and would do it, too, at any time that silence was wanted; and then encore himself and do it again; but if he was asked to sing he would go out and take a walk.

B

THE BEAR
ON THE BOAT

The tugboat gossip informed me that . . . Ben Thornburg was dead long ago; also his wild "cub," whom I used to quarrel with all through every daylight watch. A heedless, reckless creature he was, and always in hot water, always in mischief. An Arkansas passenger brought an enormous bear aboard one day, and chained him to a life-boat on the hurricane-deck. Thornburg's "cub" could not rest till he had gone there and unchained the bear, to "see what he would do." He was promptly gratified. The bear chased him around and around the deck, for miles and miles, with two hundred eager faces grinning through the railings for audience, and finally snatched off the lad's coat-tail and went into the texas to chew it. The off-watch turned out with alacrity, and left the bear in sole possession. He presently grew lonesome, and started out for recreation. He ranged the whole boat—visited every part of it, with an advance-guard of fleeing people in front of him and a voiceless vacancy behind him; and when his owner captured him at last, those two were the only visible beings anywhere; everybody else was in hiding, and the boat was a solitude.

BERMUDA SPIDERS

The birds we came across in the country were singularly tame; even that wild creature, the quail, would pick around in the grass at ease while we inspected it and talked about it at leisure. A small bird of the canary species had to be stirred up with the butt-end of the whip before it would move, and then it moved only a couple of feet. It is said that even the suspicious flea is tame and sociable in Bermuda, and will allow himself to be caught and caressed without misgivings. This should be taken with allowance, for doubtless there is more or less brag about it. In San Francisco they used to claim that their native flea could kick a child over, as if it were a merit in a flea to be able to do that; as if the knowledge of it trumpeted abroad ought to entice immigration. Such a thing in nine cases out of ten would be almost sure to deter a thinking man from coming.

We saw no bugs or reptiles to speak of, and so I was thinking of saying in print, in a general way, that there were none at all; but one night after I had gone to bed, the Reverend came into my room carrying something, and asked, "Is this your boot?" I said it was, and he said he had met a spider going off with it. Next morning he stated that just at dawn the same spider raised his window and was coming in to get a shirt, but saw him and fled.

I inquired, "Did he get the shirt?"
"No."
"How did you know it was a shirt he was after?"
"I could see it in his eye."

We inquired around, but could hear of no Bermudian spider capable of doing these things. Citizens said that their largest spiders could not more than spread their legs over an ordinary saucer, and that they had always been considered honest. Here was testimony of a clergyman against the testimony of mere worldlings—interested ones, too. On the whole, I judged it best to lock up my things.

BICYCLE DOGS

There was a row of low stepping-stones across one end of the street, a measured yard apart. Even after I got so I could steer pretty fairly I was so afraid of those stones that I always hit them. They gave me the worst falls I ever got in that street, except those which I got from dogs. I have seen it stated that no expert is quick enough to run over a dog; that a dog is always able to skip out of his way. I think that that may be true; but I think that the reason he couldn't run over the dog was because he was trying to. I did not try to run over any dog. But I ran over every dog that came along. I think it makes a great deal of difference. If you try to run over the dog he knows how to calculate, but if you are trying to miss him he does not know how to calculate and is liable to jump the wrong way every time. It was always so in my experience. Even when I could not hit a wagon I could hit a dog that came to see me practise. They all liked to see me practise, and they all came, for there was very little going on in our neighborhood to entertain a dog. It took time to learn to miss a dog, but I achieved even that.

I can steer as well as I want to, now, and I will catch that boy out one of these days and run over *him* if he doesn't reform.

Get a bicycle. You will not regret it, if you live.

THE BOAR ON THE MOUNTAIN

By and by we came to the Mauvais Pas, or the Villainous Road, to translate it feelingly. It was a breakneck path around the face of a precipice forty or fifty feet high, and nothing to hang on to but some iron railings. I got along, slowly, safely, and uncomfortably, and finally reached the middle. My hopes began to rise a little, but they were quickly blighted; for there I met a hog—a long-nosed, bristly fellow, that held up his snout and worked his nostrils at me inquiringly. A hog on a pleasure excursion in Switzerland—think of it! It is striking and unusual; a body might write a poem about it. He could not retreat, if he had been disposed to do it. It would have been foolish to stand upon our dignity in a place where there was hardly room to stand upon our feet, so we did nothing of the sort. There were twenty or thirty ladies and gentlemen behind us; we all turned about and went back, and the hog followed behind. The creature did not seem set up by what he had done; he had probably done it before.

C

CAMELS

By half past six we were under way, and all the Syrian world seemed to be under way also. The road was filled with mule-trains and long processions of camels. This reminds me that we have been trying for some time to think what a camel looks like, and now we have made it out. When he is down on all his knees, flat on his breast to receive his load, he looks something like a goose swimming; and when he is upright he looks like an ostrich with an extra set of legs. Camels are not beautiful, and their long under-lip gives them an exceedingly "gallus"[1] expression. They have immense flat, forked cushions of feet, that make a track in the dust like a pie with a slice cut out of it. They are not particular about their diet. They would eat a tombstone if they could bite it. A thistle grows about here which has needles on it that would pierce through leather, I think; if one touches you, you can find relief in nothing but profanity. The camels eat these. They show by their actions that they enjoy them. I suppose it would be a real treat to a camel to have a keg of nails for supper.

* * *

[1]Excuse the slang—no other word will describe it.
—*M.T.*

Two hours from Tabor to Nazareth—and as it was an uncommonly narrow, crooked trail, we necessarily met all the camel-trains and jackass-caravans between Jericho and Jacksonville in that particular place and nowhere else. The donkeys do not matter so much, because they are so small that you can jump your horse over them if he is an animal of spirit, but a camel is not jumpable. A camel is as tall as any ordinary dwelling-house in Syria—which is to say a camel is from one to two, and sometimes nearly three feet taller than a good-sized man. In this part of the country his load is oftenest in the shape of colossal sacks—one on each side. He and his cargo take up as much room as a carriage. Think of meeting this style of obstruction in a narrow trail. The camel would not turn out for a king. He stalks serenely along, bringing his cushioned stilts forward with the long, regular swing of a pendulum, and whatever is in the way must get out of the way peaceably, or be wiped out forcibly by the bulky sacks. It was a tiresome ride to us, and perfectly exhausting to the horses. We were compelled to jump over upward of eighteen hundred donkeys, and only one person in the party was unseated less than sixty times by the camels. This seems like a powerful statement, but the poet has said, "Things are not what they seem." I cannot think of anything now more certain to make one shudder, than to have a soft-footed camel sneak up behind him and touch him on the ear with its cold, flabby under-lip. A camel did this for one of the boys, who was drooping over his saddle in a brown-study. He glanced up and saw the majestic apparition hovering above him, and made frantic efforts to get out of the way, but the camel reached out and bit him on the shoulder before he accomplished it. This was the only pleasant incident of the journey.

CAMELS

Camels have appetites that anything will relieve temporarily, but nothing satisfy. In Syria, once, at the headwaters of the Jordan, a camel took charge of my overcoat while the tents were being pitched, and examined it with a critical eye, all over, with as much interest as if he had an idea of getting one made like it; and then, after he was done figuring on it as an article of apparel, he began to contemplate it as an article of diet. He put his foot on it, and lifted one of the sleeves out with his teeth, and chewed and chewed at it, gradually taking it in, and all

18

the while opening and closing his eyes in a kind of religious ecstasy, as if he had never tasted anything as good as an overcoat before in his life. Then he smacked his lips once or twice, and reached after the other sleeve. Next he tried the velvet collar, and smiled a smile of such contentment that it was plain to see that he regarded that as the daintiest thing about an overcoat. The tails went next, along with some percussion-caps and cough-candy, and some fig-paste from Constantinople. And then my newspaper correspondence dropped out, and he took a chance in that—manuscript letters written for the home papers. But he was treading on dangerous ground, now. He began to come across solid wisdom in those documents that was rather weighty on his stomach; and occasionally he would take a joke that would shake him up till it loosened his teeth; it was getting to be perilous times with him, but he held his grip with good courage and hopefully, till at last he began to stumble on statements that not even a camel could swallow with impunity. He began to gag and gasp, and his eyes to stand out, and his forelegs to spread, and in about a quarter of a minute he fell over as stiff as a carpenter's workbench, and died a death of indescribable agony. I went and pulled the manuscript out of his mouth, and found that the sensitive creature had choked to death on one of the mildest and gentlest statements of fact that I ever laid before a trusting public.

THE CELEBRATED JUMPING FROG OF CALAVERAS COUNTY

In compliance with the request of a friend of mine, who wrote me from the East, I called on good-natured, garrulous old Simon Wheeler, and inquired after my friend's friend, Leonidas W. Smiley, as requested to do, and I hereunto append the result. I have a lurking suspi-

cion that *Leonidas* W. Smiley is a myth; that my friend never knew such a personage; and that he only conjectured that if I asked old Wheeler about him, it would remind him of his infamous *Jim* Smiley, and he would go to work and bore me to death with some exasperating reminiscence of him as long and as tedious as it should be useless to me. If that was the design, it succeeded.

I found Simon Wheeler dozing comfortably by the bar-room stove of the dilapidated tavern in the decayed mining camp of Angel's, and I noticed that he was fat and bald-headed, and had an expression of winning gentleness and simplicity upon his tranquil countenance. He roused up, and gave me good day. I told him that a friend of mine had commissioned me to make some inquiries about a cherished companion of his boyhood named *Leonidas W.* Smiley—*Rev. Leonidas W.* Smiley, a young minister of the Gospel, who he had heard was at

one time a resident of Angel's Camp. I added that if Mr. Wheeler could tell me anything about this Rev. Leonidas W. Smiley, I would feel under many obligations to him.

Simon Wheeler backed me into a corner and blockaded me there with his chair, and then sat down and reeled off the monotonous narrative which follows this paragraph. He never smiled, he never frowned, he never changed his voice from the gentle-flowing key to which he tuned his initial sentence, he never betrayed the slightest suspicion of enthusiasm; but all through the interminable narrative there ran a vein of impressive earnestness and sincerity, which showed me plainly that, so far from his imagining that there was anything ridiculous or funny about his story, he regarded it as a really important matter, and admired its two heroes as men of transcendent genius in *finesse*. I let him go on in his own way, and never interrupted him once.

"Rev. Leonidas W. H'm, Reverend Le—well, there was a feller here once by the name of *Jim* Smiley, in the winter of '49—or maybe it was the spring of '50—I don't recollect exactly, somehow, though what makes me think it was one or the other is because I remember the big flume warn't finished when he first come to the camp; but anyway, he was the curiousest man about always betting on anything that turned up you ever see, if he could get anybody to bet on the other side; and if he couldn't he'd change sides. Any way that suited the other man would suit *him*—any way just so's he got a bet, *he* was satisfied. But still he was lucky, uncommon lucky; he most always come out winner. He was always ready and laying for a chance; there couldn't be no solit'ry thing mentioned but that feller'd offer to bet on it, and take ary side you please, as I was just telling you. If there was a horse-race, you'd find him flush or you'd find him busted at the end of it; if there was a dog-fight, he'd bet on it; if there was a cat-fight, he'd bet on it; if there was a chicken-fight, he'd bet on it; why, if there was two birds setting on a fence, he would bet you which one would fly first; or if there was a camp-meeting, he would be there reg'lar to bet on Parson Walker, which he judged to be the best exhorter about here, and so he was too, and a good man. If he even see a straddle-bug start to go anywheres, he would bet you how long it would take him to get to—to wherever he was going to, and if you took him up, he would foller that straddle-bug to Mexico but what he would find out where he was bound for and how long he was on the road. Lots of the boys here has seen that Smiley, and can tell you about him. Why, it never made no difference to *him*—he'd bet on *any* thing—the dangdest feller. Parson Walker's wife laid very sick once, for a good while, and it seemed as if they warn't going to save her; but one morning he come in, and Smiley up and asked him how she was, and he said she was considerable better—thank the Lord for his inf'nite mercy—and coming on so smart that with the blessing of Prov'dence she'd get well yet; and Smiley, before he thought, says, 'Well, I'll resk two-and-a-half she don't anyway.'

"Thish-yer Smiley had a mare—the boys called her the fifteen-minute nag, but that was only in fun, you know, because of course she was faster than that—and he used to win money on that horse, for all she was so slow and always had the asthma, or the distemper, or the consumption, or something of that kind. They used to give her two or three hundred yards' start, and then pass her under way; but always at the fag end of the race she'd get excited and desperate like, and come cavorting and straddling up, and scattering her legs around limber, sometimes in the air, and sometimes out to one side among the fences, and kicking up m-o-r-e dust and raising m-o-r-e racket with her coughing and sneezing and blowing her nose—and *always* fetch up at the stand just about a neck ahead, as near as you could cipher it down.

"And he had a little small bull-pup, that to look at him you'd think he warn't worth a cent but to set around and look ornery and lay for a chance to steal something. But as soon as money was up on him he was a different dog; his under-jaw'd begin to stick out like the fo'castle of a steamboat, and his teeth would uncover and shine like the furnaces. And a dog might tackle him and bully-rag him, and bite him, and throw him over his shoulder two or three times, and Andrew Jackson—which was the name of the pup—Andrew Jackson would never let on but what *he* was satisfied, and hadn't expected nothing else—and the bets being doubled and doubled on the other side all the time, till the money was all up; and then all of a sudden he would grab that other dog jest by the j'int of his hind leg and freeze to it—not chaw, you understand, but only just grip and hang on till they throwed up the sponge, if it was a year. Smiley always come out winner on that pup, till he harnessed a dog once that didn't have no hind legs, because they'd been sawed off in a circular saw, and when the thing had gone along far enough, and the money was all up, and he come to make a snatch for his pet holt, he see in a minute how he'd been imposed on, and how the other dog had him in the door, so to speak, and he 'peared surprised, and then he looked sorter discouraged-like, and didn't try no more to win the fight, and so he got shucked out bad. He give Smiley a look, as much as to say his heart was broke, and it was *his* fault, for putting up a dog that hadn't no hind legs for him to take holt of, which was his main dependence in a fight, and then he limped off a piece and laid down and died. It was a good pup, was that Andrew Jackson, and would have made a name for hisself if he'd lived, for the stuff was in him and he had genius—I know it, because he hadn't no opportunities to speak of, and it don't stand to reason that a dog could make such a fight as he could under them circumstances if he hadn't no talent. It always makes me feel sorry when I think of that last fight of his'n, and the way it turned out.

"Well, thish-yer Smiley had rat-tarriers, and chicken cocks, and tomcats and all them kind of things, till you couldn't rest, and you couldn't fetch nothing for him to bet on but he'd match you. He ketched a frog one day, and took him home, and said he cal'lated to educate him; and so he never done nothing for three months but set in his back yard and learn that frog to jump. And you bet you he *did* learn him, too. He'd give him a little punch behind, and the next minute you'd see that frog whirling in the air like a doughnut—see him turn one summerset, or maybe a couple, if he got a good start, and come down flat-footed and all right, like a cat. He got him up so in the matter of ketching flies, and kep' him in practice so constant, that he'd nail a fly every time as fur as he could see him. Smiley said all a frog wanted was education, and he could do 'most anything—and I believe him. Why, I've seen him set Dan'l Webster down here on this floor—Dan'l Webster was the name of the frog—and sing out, 'Flies, Dan'l, flies!' and quicker'n you could wink he'd spring straight up and snake a fly off'n the counter there, and flop down on the floor ag'in as solid as a gob of mud, and fall to scratching the side of his head with his hind foot as indifferent as if he hadn't no idea he'd been doin' any more'n any frog might do. You never see a frog so modest and straightfor'ard as he was, for all he was so gifted. And when it come to fair and square jumping on a dead level, he could get over more ground at one straddle than any animal of his breed you ever see. Jumping on a dead level was his strong suit, you understand; and when it come to that, Smiley would ante up money on him as long as he had a red. Smiley was monstrous proud of his frog, and well he might be, for fellers that had traveled and been everywheres all said he laid over any frog that ever *they* see.

"Well, Smiley kep' the beast in a little lattice box, and

he used to fetch him down-town sometimes and lay for a bet. One day a feller—a stranger in the camp, he was—come acrost him with his box, and says:

" 'What might it be that you've got in the box?'

"And Smiley says, sorter indifferent-like, 'It might be a parrot, or it might be a canary, maybe, but it ain't—it's only just a frog.'

"And the feller took it, and looked at it careful, and turned it round this way and that, and says, 'H'm—so 'tis. Well, what's *he* good for?'

" 'Well,' Smiley says, easy and careless, 'he's good enough for *one* thing, I should judge—he can outjump any frog in Calaveras County.'

"The feller took the box again, and took another long, particular look, and give it back to Smiley, and says, very deliberate, 'Well,' he says, 'I don't see no p'ints about that frog that's any better'n any other frog.'

" 'Maybe you don't,' Smiley says. 'Maybe you understand frogs and maybe you don't understand 'em; maybe you've had experience, and maybe you ain't only a amature, as it were. Anyways, I've got *my* opinion, and I'll resk forty dollars that he can outjump any frog in Calaveras County.'

"And the feller studied a minute, and then says, kinder sad-like, 'Well, I'm only a stranger here, and I ain't got no frog; but if I had a frog, I'd bet you.'

"And then Smiley says, 'That's all right—that's all right—if you'll hold my box a minute, I'll go and get you a frog.' And so the feller took the box, and put up his forty dollars along with Smiley's, and set down to wait.

"So he set there a good while thinking and thinking to himself, and then he got the frog out and prized his mouth open and took a teaspoon and filled him full of quail-shot—filled him pretty near up to his chin—and set him on the floor. Smiley he went to the swamp and slopped around in the mud for a long time, and finally he ketched a frog, and fetched him in, and give him to this feller, and says:

" 'Now, if you're ready, set him alongside of Dan'l, with his fore paws just even with Dan'l's, and I'll give the word.' Then he says, 'One—two—three—*git!*' and him and the feller touched up the frogs from behind, and the new frog hopped off lively, but Dan'l give a heave, and hysted up his shoulders—so—like a Frenchman, but it warn't no use—he couldn't budge; he was planted as solid as a church, and he couldn't no more stir than if he was anchored out. Smiley was a good deal surprised, and he was disgusted too, but he didn't have no idea what the matter was, of course.

"The feller took the money and started away; and when he was going out at the door, he sorter jerked his thumb over his shoulder—so—at Dan'l, and says again, very deliberate, 'Well,' he says, 'I don't see no p'ints about that frog that's any better'n any other frog.'

"Smiley he stood scratching his head and looking down at Dan'l a long time, and at last he says, 'I do wonder what in the nation that frog throw'd off for—I wonder if there ain't something the matter with him—he 'pears to look mighty baggy, somehow.' And he ketched Dan'l by the nap of the neck, and hefted him, and says, 'Why blame my cats if he don't weigh five pound!' and turned him upside down and he belched out a double handful of shot. And then he see how it was, and he was the maddest man—he set the frog down and took out after that feller, but he never ketched him. And—"

[Here Simon Wheeler heard his name called from the front yard, and got up to see what was wanted.] And turning to me as he moved away, he said: "Just set where you are, stranger, and rest easy—I ain't going to be gone a second."

But, by your leave, I did not think that a continuation of the history of the enterprising vagabond *Jim* Smiley would be likely to afford me much information concerning the Rev. *Leonidas W.* Smiley, and so I started away.

At the door I met the sociable Wheeler returning, and he buttonholed me and recommenced:

"Well, thish-yer Smiley had a yaller one-eyed cow that didn't have no tail, only just a short stump like a bannanner, and—"

However, lacking both time and inclination, I did not wait to hear about the afflicted cow, but took my leave.

THE CHAMELEON

He is fat and indolent and contemplative; but is businesslike and capable when a fly comes about—reaches out a tongue like a teaspoon and takes him in. He gums his tongue first. He is always pious, in his looks. And pious and thankful both when Providence or one of us sends him a fly. He has a froggy head, and a back like a new grave—for shape; and hands like a bird's toes that have

been frost-bitten. But his eyes are his exhibition feature. A couple of skinny cones project from the sides of his head, with a wee shiny bead of an eye set in the apex of each; and these cones turn bodily like pivot-guns and point every which way, and they are independent of each other; each has its own exclusive machinery. When I am behind him and C. in front of him, he whirls one eye rearward and the other forward—which gives him a most Congressional expression (one eye on the constituency and one on the swag); and then if something happens above and below him he shoots out one eye upward like a telescope and the other downward—and this changes his expression, but does not improve it.

THE COBRA

It will be perceived that the snakes are not much interested in cattle; they kill only 3,000 odd per year. The snakes are much more interested in man. India swarms with deadly snakes. At the head of the list is the cobra, the deadliest known to the world, a snake whose bite kills where the rattlesnake's bite merely entertains. . . . There are narrow escapes in India. In the very jungle where I killed sixteen tigers and all those elephants, a cobra bit

me, but it got well; every one was surprised. This could not happen twice in ten years, perhaps. Usually death would result in fifteen minutes.

THE COYOTE

Along about an hour after breakfast we saw the first prairie-dog villages, the first antelope, and the first wolf. If I remember rightly, this latter was the regular *coyote* (pronounced ky-*o*-te) *of the farther deserts*. And if it was, he was not a pretty creature, or respectable either, for I got well acquainted with his race afterward, and can speak with confidence. The coyote is a long, slim, sick and sorry-looking skeleton, with a gray wolf-skin stretched over it, a tolerably bushy tail that forever sags down with a despairing expression of forsakenness and misery, a furtive and evil eye, and a long, sharp face, with slightly lifted lip and exposed teeth. He has a general slinking expression all over. The coyote is a living, breathing allegory of Want. He is *always* hungry. He is always poor, out of luck and friendless. The meanest creatures despise him, and even the fleas would desert him for a velocipede. He is so spiritless and cowardly that even while his exposed teeth are pretending a threat, the rest of his face is apologizing for it. And he is *so* homely!—so scrawny, and ribby, and coarse-haired, and pitiful. When he sees you he lifts his lip and lets a flash of his teeth out, and then turns a little out of the course he was pursuing, depresses his head a bit, and strikes a long, soft-footed trot through the sage-brush, glancing over his shoulder at you, from time to time, till he is about out of easy pistol range, and then he stops and takes a deliberate survey of you; he will trot fifty yards and stop again—another fifty and stop again; and finally the gray of his gliding body blends with the gray of the sage-brush, and he disappears. All this is when you make no demonstration against him; but if you do, he develops a livelier interest in his journey, and instantly electrifies his heels and puts such a deal of real estate between himself and your weapon, that by the time you have raised the hammer you see that you need a minie rifle, and by the time you have got him in line you need a rifled cannon, and by the time you have "drawn a bead" on him you see well enough that nothing but an unusually long-winded streak of lightning could reach him where he is now. But if you start a swift-footed dog after him, you will enjoy it ever so much—especially if it is a dog that has a good opinion of himself, and has been brought up to think he knows something about speed. The coyote will go swinging gently off on that deceitful trot of his, and every little while he will smile a fraudful smile over his shoulder that will fill that dog entirely full of encouragement and worldly ambition, and make him lay his head still lower to the ground, and stretch his neck further to the front, and pant more fiercely, and stick his tail out straighter behind, and move his furious legs with a yet wilder frenzy, and leave a broader and broader, and higher and denser cloud of desert sand smoking behind, and marking his long wake across the level plain! And all this time the dog is only a short twenty feet behind the coyote, and to save the soul of him he cannot understand why it is that he cannot get perceptibly closer; and he begins to get aggravated, and it makes him madder and madder to see how gently the coyote glides along and never pants or sweats or ceases to smile; and he grows still more and more incensed to see how shamefully he has been taken in by an entire stranger, and what an ignoble swindle that long, calm, soft-footed trot is; and next he notices that he is getting fagged, and that the coyote actually has to slacken speed a little to keep from running away from him—and *then* that town-dog is mad in earnest, and he begins to strain and weep and swear, and paw the sand higher than ever, and reach for the coyote with concentrated and desperate energy. This "spurt" finds him six feet behind the gliding enemy, and two miles from his friends. And then, in the instant that a wild new hope is lighting up his face, the coyote turns and smiles blandly upon him once more, and with a something about it which seems to say: "Well, I shall have to tear myself away from you, bub—business is business, and it will not do for me to be fooling along this way all day"—and forthwith there is a rushing sound, and the sudden splitting of a long crack through the atmosphere, and behold that dog is solitary and alone in the midst of a vast solitude!

It makes his head swim. He stops, and looks all around; climbs the nearest sand-mound, and gazes into the distance; shakes his head reflectively, and then, without a word, he turns and jogs along back to his train, and takes up a humble position under the hindmost wagon, and feels unspeakably mean, and looks ashamed, and hangs his tail at half-mast for a week. And for as much as a year after that, whenever there is a great hue and cry after a coyote, that dog will merely glance in that direction without emotion, and apparently observe to himself, "I believe I do not wish any of the pie."

The coyote lives chiefly in the most desolate and forbidding deserts, along with the lizard, the jackass-rabbit and the raven, and gets an uncertain and precarious living, and earns it. He seems to subsist almost wholly on the carcasses of oxen, mules, and horses that have dropped out of emigrant trains and died, and upon windfalls of carrion, and occasional legacies of ˙offal bequeathed to him by white men who have been opulent enough to have something better to butcher than condemned army bacon. . . .

We soon learned to recognize the sharp, vicious bark of the coyote as it came across the murky plain at night to disturb our dreams among the mail-sacks; and remembering his forlorn aspect and his hard fortune, made shift to wish him the blessed novelty of a long day's good luck and a limitless larder the morrow.

D

THE DACHSHUND

In the train, during a part of the return journey from Baroda, we had the company of a gentleman who had with him a remarkable-looking dog. I had not seen one of its kind before, as far as I could remember; though of course I might have seen one and not noticed it, for I am not acquainted with dogs, but only with cats. This dog's coat was smooth and shiny and black, and I think it had tan trimmings around the edges of the dog, and perhaps underneath. It was a long, low dog, with very short, strange legs—legs that curved inboard, something like parentheses turned the wrong way (. Indeed, it was made on the plan of a bench for length and lowness. It seemed to be satisfied, but I thought the plan poor, and structurally weak, on account of the distance between the forward supports and those abaft. With age the dog's back was likely to sag; and it seemed to me that it would have been a stronger and more practicable dog if it had had some more legs. It had not begun to sag yet, but the shape of the legs showed that the undue weight imposed upon them was beginning to tell. It had a long nose, and floppy ears that hung down, and a resigned expression of countenance. I did not like to ask what kind of a dog it was, or how it came to be deformed, for it was plain that the gentleman was very fond of it, and naturally he could be sensitive about it. From delicacy I thought it best not to seem to notice it too much. No doubt a man with a dog like that feels just as a person does who has a child that is out of true. The gentleman was not merely fond of the dog, he was also proud of it—just the same, again, as a mother feels about her child when it is an idiot. I could see that he was proud of it, notwithstanding it was such a long dog and looked so resigned and pious. It had been all over the world with him, and had been pilgriming like that for years and years. It had traveled fifty thousand miles by sea and rail, and had ridden in front of him on his horse eight thousand. It had a silver medal from the Geographical Society of Great Britain for its travels, and I saw it. It had won prizes in dog-shows, both in India and in England—I saw them.

He said its pedigree was on record in the Kennel Club, and that it was a well-known dog. He said a great many people in London could recognize it the moment they saw it. I did not say anything, but I did not think it anything strange; I should know that dog again, myself, yet I am not careful about noticing dogs. He said that when he walked along in London, people often stopped and looked at the dog. Of course I did not say anything, for I did not want to hurt his feelings, but I could have explained to him that if you take a great long low dog like that and waddle it along the street anywhere in the world and not charge anything, people will stop and look. He was gratified because the dog took prizes. But that was

nothing; if I were built like that I could take prizes myself. I wished I knew what kind of a dog it was, and what it was for, but I could not very well ask, for that would show that I did not know. Not that I want a dog like that, but only to know the secret of its birth.

I think he was going to hunt elephants with it, because I know, from remarks dropped by him, that he has hunted large game in India and Africa, and likes it. But I think that if he tries to hunt elephants with it, he is going to be disappointed. I do not believe that it is suited for elephants. It lacks energy, it lacks force of character, it lacks bitterness. These things all show in the meekness and resignation of its expression. It would not attack an elephant, I am sure of it. It might not run if it saw one coming, but it looked to me like a dog that would sit down and pray.

DELHI MONKEYS

We had a refreshing rest, there in Delhi, in a great old mansion which possessed historical interest. It was built by a rich Englishman who had become orientalized—so much so that he had a zenana. But he was a broad-minded man, and remained so. To please his harem he built a

monkeys; and they are monkeys of a watchful and enterprising sort, and not much troubled with fear. They invade the house whenever they get a chance, and carry off everything they don't want. One morning the master of the house was in his bath, and the window was open. Near it stood a pot of yellow paint and a brush. Some monkeys appeared in the window; to scare them away, the gentleman threw his sponge at them. They did not scare at all; they jumped into the room and threw yellow paint all over him from the brush, and drove him out; then they painted the walls and the floor and the tank and the windows and the furniture yellow, and were in the dressing-room painting that when help arrived and routed them.

Two of these creatures came into my room in the early morning, through a window whose shutters I had left open, and when I woke one of them was before the glass brushing his hair, and the other one had my note-book, and was reading a page of humorous notes and crying. I did not mind the one with the hair-brush, but the conduct of the other one hurt me; it hurts me yet. I threw something at him, and that was wrong, for my host had told me that the monkeys were best left alone. They threw everything at me that they could lift, and then went into the bathroom to get some more things, and I shut the door on them.

mosque; to please himself he built an English church. That kind of a man will arrive somewhere. In the Mutiny days the mansion was the British general's headquarters. It stands in a great garden—oriental fashion—and about it are many noble trees. The trees harbor

THE DINGO

. . . I also saw the wild Australian dog—the dingo. He was a beautiful creature—shapely, graceful, a little wolfish in some of his aspects, but with a most friendly eye and sociable disposition. The dingo is not an importation; he was present in great force when the whites first came to the continent. It may be that he is the oldest dog in the universe; his origin, his descent, the place where his ancestors first appeared, are as unknown and as untraceable as are the camel's. He is the most precious dog in the world, for he does not bark. But in an evil hour he got to raiding the sheep-runs to appease his hunger, and that sealed his doom. He is hunted, now, just as if he were a wolf. He has been sentenced to extermination, and the sentence will be carried out. This is all right, and not objectionable. The world was made for man—the white man.

E

THE EARL AND THE ANACONDA

Some of my experiments [as to the descent of man from the higher animals] were quite curious. In the course of my reading I had come across a case where, many years ago, some hunters on our Great Plains organized a buffalo hunt for the entertainment of an English earl—that, and to provide some fresh meat for his larder. They had charming sport. They killed seventy-two of those great animals; and ate part of one of them and left the seventy-one to rot. In order to determine the difference between an anaconda and an earl—if any—I caused seven young calves to be turned into the anaconda's cage. The grateful reptile immediately crushed one of them and swallowed it, then lay back satisfied. It showed no further interest in the calves, and no disposition to harm them. I tried this experiment with other anacondas; always with the same result. The fact stood proven that the difference between an earl and an anaconda is that the earl is cruel and the anaconda isn't; and that the earl wantonly destroys what he has no use for, but the anaconda doesn't. This seemed to suggest that the anaconda was not descended from the earl. It also seemed to suggest that the earl was descended from the anaconda, and had lost a great deal in the transition.

ELEPHANTS
OF LAHORE

We wandered contentedly around here and there in India; to Lahore, among other places, where the Lieutenant-Governor lent me an elephant. This hospitality stands out in my experiences in a stately isolation. It was a fine elephant, affable, gentlemanly, educated, and I was not afraid of it. I even rode it with confidence through the crowded lanes of the native city, where it scared all the horses out of their senses, and where children were always just escaping its feet. It took the middle of the road in a fine, independent way, and left it to the world to get out of the way or take the consequences. I am used to being afraid of collisions when I ride or drive, but when one is on top of an elephant that feeling is absent. I could have ridden in comfort through a regiment of runaway teams. I could easily learn to prefer an elephant to any other vehicle, partly because of that immunity from collisions, and partly because of the fine view one has from up there, and partly because of the dignity one feels in that high place, and partly because one can look in at the windows and see what is going on privately among the family. The Lahore horses were used to elephants, but they were rapturously afraid of them just the same. It seemed curious. Perhaps the better they know the elephant the more they respect him in that peculiar way. In our own case we are not afraid of dynamite till we get acquainted with it.

EVE FIGURES OUT HOW MILK GETS INTO THE COW

I scored the next great triumph for science myself: to wit, how the milk gets into the cow. Both of us had marveled over that mystery a long time. We had followed the cows around for years—that is, in the daytime—but had never caught them drinking a fluid of that color. And so, at last we said they undoubtedly procured it at night. Then we took turns and watched them by night. The result was the same—the puzzle remained unsolved. These proceedings were of a sort to be expected in beginners, but one perceives, now, that they were unscientific. A time came when experience had taught us better methods. One night as I lay musing, and looking at the stars, a grand idea flashed through my head, and I saw my way! My first impulse was to wake Adam and tell him, but I resisted it and kept my secret. I slept no wink the rest of the night. The moment the first pale streak of dawn appeared I flitted stealthily away; and deep in the woods I chose a small grassy spot and wattled it in, making a secure pen; then I enclosed a cow in it. I milked her dry, then left her there, a prisoner. There was nothing there to drink—she must get milk by her secret alchemy, or stay dry.

All day I was in a fidget, and could not talk connectedly I was so preoccupied; but Adam was busy trying to invent a multiplication table, and did not notice. Toward sunset he had got as far as 6 times 9 are 27, and while he was drunk with the joy of his achievement and dead to my presence and all things else, I stole away to

my cow. My hand shook so with excitement and with dread of failure that for some moments I could not get a grip on a teat; then I succeeded, and the milk came! Two gallons. Two gallons, and nothing to make it out of. I knew at once the explanation: *the milk was not taken in by the mouth, it was condensed from the atmosphere through the cow's hair.* I ran and told Adam, and his happiness was as great as mine, and his pride in me inexpressible.

F

A FABLE

Once upon a time an artist who had painted a small and very beautiful picture placed it so that he could see it in the mirror. He said, "This doubles the distance and softens it, and it is twice as lovely as it was before."

The animals out in the woods heard of this through the housecat, who was greatly admired by them because he was so learned, and so refined and civilized, and so polite and high-bred, and could tell them so much which they didn't know before, and were not certain about afterward. They were much excited about this new piece of gossip, and they asked questions, so as to get at a full understanding of it. They asked what a picture was, and the cat explained.

"It is a flat thing," he said; "wonderfully flat, marvelously flat, enchantingly flat and elegant. And, oh, so beautiful!"

That excited them almost to a frenzy, and they said they would give the world to see it. Then the bear asked:

"What is it that makes it so beautiful?"

"It is the looks of it," said the cat.

This filled them with admiration and uncertainty, and they were more excited than ever. Then the cow asked:

"What is a mirror?"

"It is a hole in the wall," said the cat. "You look in it,

and there you see the picture, and it is so dainty and charming and ethereal and inspiring in its unimaginable beauty that your head turns round and round, and you almost swoon with ecstasy."

The ass had not said anything as yet; he now began to throw doubts. He said there had never been anything as beautiful as this before, and probably wasn't now. He said that when it took a whole basketful of sesquipedalian adjectives to whoop up a thing of beauty, it was time for suspicion.

It was easy to see that these doubts were having an effect upon the animals, so the cat went off offended. The subject was dropped for a couple of days, but in the meantime curiosity was taking a fresh start, and there was a revival of interest perceptible. Then the animals assailed the ass for spoiling what could possibly have been a pleasure to them, on a mere suspicion that the picture was not beautiful, without any evidence that such was the case. The ass was not troubled; he was calm, and said there was one way to find out who was in the right, himself or the cat: he would go and look in that hole, and come back and tell what he found there. The animals felt relieved and grateful, and asked him to go at once—which he did.

But he did not know where he ought to stand; and so, through error, he stood between the picture and the mirror. The result was that the picture had no chance, and didn't show up. He returned home and said:

"The cat lied. There was nothing in that hole but an ass. There wasn't a sign of a flat thing visible. It was a handsome ass, and friendly, but just an ass, and nothing more."

The elephant asked:

"Did you see it good and clear? Were you close to it?"

"I saw it good and clear, O Hathi, King of Beasts. I was so close that I touched noses with it."

"This is very strange," said the elephant; "the cat was always truthful before—as far as we could make out. Let another witness try. Go, Baloo, look in the hole, and come and report."

So the bear went. When he came back, he said:

"Both the cat and the ass have lied; there was nothing in the hole but a bear."

Great was the surprise and puzzlement of the animals. Each was now anxious to make the test himself and get at the straight truth. The elephant sent them one at a time.

First, the cow. She found nothing in the hole but a cow.

The tiger found nothing in it but a tiger.

The lion found nothing in it but a lion.

The leopard found nothing in it but a leopard.

The camel found a camel, and nothing more.

Then Hathi was wroth, and said he would have the truth, if he had to go and fetch it himself. When he returned, he abused his whole subjectry for liars, and was in an unappeasable fury with the moral and mental blindness of the cat. He said that anybody but a near-sighted fool could see that there was nothing in the hole but an elephant.

MORAL, BY THE CAT

You can find in a text whatever you bring, if you will stand between it and the mirror of your imagination. You may not see your ears, but they will be there.

FLORENTINE FLIES

Sept. 29, '92.—I seem able to forget everything except that I have had my head shaved. No matter how closely I shut myself away from draughts it seems to be always breezy up there. But the main difficulty is the flies. They like it up there better than anywhere else; on account of the view, I suppose. It seems to me that I have never seen any flies before that were shod like these. These appear to have talons. Wherever they put their foot down they grab. They walk over my head all the time and cause me infinite torture. It is their park, their club, their summer resort. They have garden parties there, and conventions, and all sorts of dissipation. And they fear nothing. All flies are daring, but these are more daring than those of other nationalities. These cannot be scared away by any device. They are more diligent, too, than the other kinds; they come before daylight and stay till after dark.

G

THE GENUINE MEXICAN PLUG

I resolved to have a horse to ride. I had never seen such wild, free, magnificent horsemanship outside of a circus as these picturesquely clad Mexicans, Californians, and Mexicanized Americans displayed in Carson streets every day. How they rode! Leaning just gently forward out of the perpendicular, easy and nonchalant, with broad slouchhat brim blown square up in front, and long *riata* swinging above the head, they swept through the town like the wind! The next minute they were only a sailing puff of dust on the far desert. If they trotted, they sat up gallantly and gracefully, and seemed part of the horse; did not go jiggering up and down after the silly Miss-Nancy fashion of the riding-schools. I had quickly learned to tell a horse from a cow, and was full of anxiety to learn more. I was resolved to buy a horse.

While the thought was rankling in my mind, the auctioneer came scurrying through the plaza on a black beast that had as many humps and corners on him as a dromedary, and was necessarily uncomely; but he was "going, at twenty-two!—horse, saddle and bridle at twenty-two dollars, gentlemen!" and I could hardly resist.

A man whom I did not know (he turned out to be the auctioneer's brother) noticed the wistful look in my eye, and observed that that was a very remarkable horse to be going at such a price; and added that the saddle alone was worth the money. It was a Spanish saddle, with ponderous *tapidaros*, and furnished with the ungainly sole-leather covering with the unspellable name. I said I had half a notion to bid. Then this keen-eyed person appeared to me to be "taking my measure"; but I dismissed the suspicion when he spoke, for his manner was full of guileless candor and truthfulness. Said he:

"I know that horse—know him well. You are a stranger, I take it, and so you might think he was an American horse, maybe, but I assure you he is not. He is nothing of the kind; but—excuse my speaking in a low voice, other people being near—he is, without the shadow of a doubt, a Genuine Mexican Plug!"

I did not know what a Genuine Mexican Plug was, but there was something about this man's way of saying it, that made me swear inwardly that I would own a Genuine Mexican Plug, or die.

"Has he any other—er—advantages?" I inquired, suppressing what eagerness I could.

again, and came down on the horse's neck—all in the space of three or four seconds. Then he rose and stood almost straight up on his hind feet, and I, clasping his lean neck desperately, slid back into the saddle, and held on. He came down, and immediately hoisted his heels into the air, delivering a vicious kick at the sky, and stood on his fore feet. And then down he came once more, and began the original exercise of shooting me straight up again.

The third time I went up I heard a stranger say: "Oh, *don't* he buck, though!"

While I was up, somebody struck the horse a sounding thwack with a leathern strap, and when I arrived again the Genuine Mexican Plug was not there. A Californian youth chased him up and caught him, and asked if he might have a ride. I granted him that luxury. He mounted the Genuine, got lifted into the air once, but sent his spurs home as he descended, and the horse darted away like a telegram. He soared over three fences like a bird, and disappeared down the road toward the Washoe Valley.

I sat down on a stone with a sigh, and by a natural impulse one of my hands sought my forehead, and the other the base of my stomach. I believe I never appreciated, till then, the poverty of the human machinery—for I still needed a hand or two to place elsewhere. Pen cannot describe how I was jolted up. Imagination cannot conceive how disjointed I was—how internally, externally, and universally I was unsettled, mixed up, and ruptured. There was a sympathetic crowd around me, though.

One elderly-looking comforter said:

"Stranger, you've been taken in. Everybody in this camp knows that horse. Any child, any Injun, could have told you that he'd buck; he is the very worst devil to buck on the continent of America. You hear *me*. I'm Curry. *Old* Curry. Old *Abe* Curry. And moreover, he is a simon-pure, out-and-out, genuine d—d Mexican plug, and an uncommon mean one at that, too. Why, you turnip, if you had laid low and kept dark, there's chances to buy an *American* horse for mighty little more than you paid for that bloody old foreign relic."

I gave no sign; but I made up my mind that if the auctioneer's brother's funeral took place while I was in the territory I would postpone all other recreations and attend it.

He hooked his forefinger in the pocket of my army shirt, led me to one side, and breathed in my ear impressively these words:

"He can out-buck anything in America!"

"Going, going, going—at *twent-ty*-four dollars and ahalf, gen—" "Twenty-seven!" I shouted, in a frenzy.

"And sold!" said the auctioneer, and passed over the Genuine Mexican Plug to me.

I could scarcely contain my exultation. I paid the money, and put the animal in a neighboring livery stable to dine and rest himself.

In the afternoon I brought the creature into the plaza,

and certain citizens held him by the head, and others by the tail, while I mounted him. As soon as they let go, he placed all his feet in a bunch together, lowered his back, and then suddenly arched it upward, and shot me straight into the air a matter of three or four feet! I came as straight down again, lit in the saddle, went instantly up again, came down almost on the high pommel, shot up

GREAT GRANDFATHER THE GORILLA

21 Fifth Ave., New York,
November 14, 1905.

DEAR MR. ROW,—That alleged portrait has a private history. Napoleon Sarony* was as much of an enthusiast about wild animals as he was about photography; and when Du Chaillu brought the first Gorilla to this country in 1819 he came to me in a fever of excitement and asked me if my father was of record and authentic. I said he was; then Sarony, without any abatement of his excitement, asked if my grandfather also was of record and authentic. I said he was. Then Sarony, with still rising excitement and with joy added to it, said he had found my great grandfather in the person of the gorilla and had recognized him at once by his resemblance to me. I was deeply hurt but did not reveal this, because I knew Sarony meant no offense for the gorilla had not done him any harm, and he was not a man who would say an unkind thing about a gorilla wantonly. I went with him to inspect the ancestor, and examined him from several points of view, without being able to detect anything more than a passing resemblance. "Wait," said Sarony with strong confidence, "let me show you." He borrowed my overcoat and put it on the gorilla. The result was surprising. I saw that the gorilla while not looking distinctly like me was exactly what my great grandfather would have looked like if I had had one. Sarony photographed the creature in that overcoat, and spread the picture about the world. It has remained spread about the world ever since. It turns up every week in some newspaper somewhere or other. It is not my favorite, but to my exasperation it is everybody else's. Do you think you could get it suppressed for me? I will pay the limit.

Sincerely yours,

S. L. CLEMENS.

*A fashionable and "artistic" photographer of the period who had published what Mark Twain considered an execrable portrait of him.—ED.

H

THE HOOT OWL

When a cackling hen is far away and is saying K-k-k-k-k-k KWACKO! you hear nothing but the first syllable of her last word—just a single strenuous note, pitched on a high key, all the rest is lost in the intervening distance. At a distance this fiend-owl's note sounds like that. Close by it is soft and dovelike and it is not so very unlike a flute note. It is quadruple time—one utterance to the bar, followed by three quarter-note rests, thus h-o-o-o h-o-o-o   h-o-o-o o   h-o-o-o-o
The monotony of it is maddening. You beat time to it, and count the hoots and the rests—you cannot help it. You count till your reason reels. Low and soft as the note is, it is marvelously penetrating; it bores into the skull like an auger. It can distress you when it is 150 yards away; at a third of that distance it is unendurable. When you have counted fifty hoots and 150 rests you have reached the limit of human endurance. You must turn and drive the creature away or your mind will go to ruin.

THE HOUND PUP

We four always spread our common stock of blankets together on the frozen ground, and slept side by side; and finding that our foolish, long-legged hound pup had a deal of animal heat in him, Oliphant got to admitting him to the bed, between himself and Mr. Ballou, hugging the dog's warm back to his breast and finding great comfort in it. But in the night the pup would get stretchy and brace his feet against the old man's back and shove, grunting complacently the while; and now and then, being warm and snug, grateful and happy, he would paw the old man's back simply in excess of comfort; and at yet other times he would dream of the chase and in his sleep tug at the old man's back hair and bark in his ear. The old gentleman complained mildly about these familiarities, at last, and when he got through with his statement he said that such a dog as that was not a proper animal to admit to bed with tired men, because he was "so meretricious in his movements and so organic in his emotions." We turned the dog out.

HUNTING THE DECEITFUL TURKEY

When I was a boy my uncle and his big boys hunted with the rifle, the youngest boy Fred and I with a shotgun—a small single-barrelled shotgun which was properly suited to our size and strength; it was not much heavier than a broom. We carried it turn about, half an hour at a time. I was not able to hit anything with it, but I liked to try. Fred and I hunted feathered small game, the others hunted deer, squirrels, wild turkeys, and such things. My uncle and the big boys were good shots. They killed hawks and wild geese and such like on the wing; and they didn't wound or kill squirrels, they *stunned* them. When the dogs treed a squirrel, the squirrel would scamper aloft and run out on a limb and flatten himself along it, hoping to make himself invisible in that way—and not quite succeeding. You could see his wee little ears sticking up. You couldn't see his nose, but you knew where it was. Then the hunter, despising a "rest" for his rifle, stood up and took offhand aim at the limb and sent a bullet into it immediately under the squirrel's nose, and down tumbled the animal, unwounded but unconscious; the dogs gave him a shake and he was dead. Sometimes when the distance was great and the wind not accurately allowed for, the bullet would hit the squirrel's head; the dogs could do as they pleased with that one—the hunter's pride was hurt, and he wouldn't allow it to go into the game-bag.

In the first faint gray of the dawn the stately wild turkeys would be stalking around in great flocks, and ready to be sociable and answer invitations to come and converse with other excursionists of their kind. The hunter concealed himself and imitated the turkey-call by sucking the air through the legbone of a turkey which had previously answered a call like that and lived only just long enough to regret it. There is nothing that furnishes a perfect turkey-call except that bone. Another of Nature's treacheries, you see. She is full of them; half the time she doesn't know which she likes best—to betray her child or protect it. In the case of the turkey she is badly mixed: she gives it a bone to be used in getting it into trouble, and she also furnishes it with a trick for getting itself out of the trouble again. When a mamma-turkey answers an invitation and finds she has made a mistake in accepting it, she does as the mamma-partridge does— remembers a previous engagement and goes limping and scrambling away, pretending to be very lame; and at the same time she is saying to her not-visible children, "Lie low, keep still, don't expose yourselves; I shall be back as soon as I have beguiled this shabby swindler out of the country."

When a person is ignorant and confiding, this immoral device can have tiresome results. I followed an ostensibly lame turkey over a considerable part of the United States one morning, because I believed in her and could not think she would deceive a mere boy, and one who was trusting her and considering her honest. I had the single-barrelled shotgun, but my idea was to catch her alive. I often got within rushing distance of her, and then made my rush; but always, just as I made my final plunge and put my hand down where her back had been, it wasn't there; it was only two or three inches from there and I brushed the tail-feathers as I landed on my stomach—a very close call, but still not quite close enough; that is, not close enough for success, but just close enough to convince me that I could do it next time. She always waited for me, a little piece away, and let on to be resting and greatly fatigued; which was a lie, but I believed it, for I still thought her honest long after I ought to have begun to doubt her, suspecting that this was no way for a high-minded bird to be acting. I followed, and followed, and followed, making my periodical rushes, and getting up and brushing the dust off, and resuming the voyage with patient confidence; indeed, with a confidence which grew, for I could see by the change of climate and vegetation that we were getting up into the high latitudes, and as she always looked a little tireder and a little more discouraged after each rush, I judged that I was safe to win, in the end, the competition being purely a matter of staying power and the advantage lying with me from the start because she was lame.

Along in the afternoon I began to feel fatigued myself. Neither of us had had any rest since we first started on the excursion, which was upwards of ten hours before, though latterly we had paused awhile after rushes, I letting·on to be thinking about something else; but neither of us sincere, and both of us waiting for the other to call game but in no real hurry about it, for indeed those little evanescent snatches of rest were very grateful to the feelings of us both; it would naturally be so, skirmishing along like that ever since dawn and not a bite in the meantime; at least for me, though sometimes as she lay on her side fanning herself with a wing and praying for strength to get out of this difficulty a grasshopper happened along whose time had come, and that was well for her, and fortunate, but I had nothing—nothing the whole day.

More than once, after I was very tired, I gave up taking her alive, and was going to shoot her, but I never did it, although it was my right, for I did not believe I could hit her; and besides, she always stopped and posed, when I raised the gun, and this made me suspicious that she knew about me and my marksmanship, and so I did not care to expose myself to remarks.

I did not get her, at all. When she got tired of the game at last, she rose from almost under my hand and flew aloft with the rush and whir of a shell and lit on the highest limb of a great tree and sat down and crossed her legs and smiled down at me, and seemed gratified to see me so astonished.

I was ashamed, and also lost; and it was while wandering the woods hunting for myself that I found a deserted log cabin and had one of the best meals there that in my life-days I have eaten. The weed-grown garden was full of ripe tomatoes, and I ate them ravenously, though I had never liked them before. Not more than two or three times since have I tasted anything that was so delicious as those tomatoes. I surfeited myself with them, and did not taste another one until I was in middle life. I can eat them now, but I do not like the look of them. I suppose we have all experienced a surfeit at one time or another. Once, in stress of circumstances, I ate part of a barrel of sardines, there being nothing else at hand, but since then I have always been able to get along without sardines.

I

THE INDIAN CROW

By midnight I had suffered all the different kinds of shocks there are, and knew that I could never more be disturbed by them, either isolated or in combination. Then came peace—stillness deep and solemn—and lasted till five.

Then it all broke loose again. And who restarted it? The Bird of Birds—the Indian crow. I came to know him well, by and by, and be infatuated with him. I suppose he is the hardest lot that wears feathers. Yes, and the cheerfulest, and the best satisfied with himself. He never arrived at what he is by any careless process, or any sudden one; he is a work of art, and "art is long"; he is the product of immemorial ages, and of deep calculation; one can't make a bird like that in a day. He has been reincarnated more times than Shiva; and he has kept a sample of each incarnation, and fused it into his constitution. In the course of his evolutionary promotions, his sublime march toward ultimate perfection, he has been a gambler, a low comedian, a dissolute priest, a fussy woman, a blackguard, a scoffer, a liar, a thief, a spy, an informer, a trading politician, a swindler, a professional hypocrite, a patriot for cash, a reformer, a lecturer, a lawyer, a conspirator, a rebel, a royalist, a democrat, a practicer and propagator of irreverence, a meddler, an intruder, a busybody, an infidel, and a wallower in sin for the mere love of it. The strange result, the incredible result, of this patient accumulation of all damnable traits is, that he does not know what care is, he does not know what sorrow is, he does not know what remorse is; his life is one long thundering ecstasy of happiness, and he will go to his death untroubled, knowing that he will soon turn up again as an author or something, and be even more intolerably capable and comfortable than ever he was before.

In his straddling wide forward-step, and his springy sidewise series of hops, and his impudent air, and his cunning way of canting his head to one side upon occasion, he reminds one of the American blackbird. But the sharp resemblances stop there. He is much bigger than the blackbird; and he lacks the blackbird's trim and slender and beautiful build and shapely beak; and of course his sober garb of gray and rusty black is a poor and humble thing compared with the splendid luster of the blackbird's metallic sables and shifting and flashing bronze glories. The blackbird is a perfect gentleman, in deportment and attire, and is not noisy, I believe, except when holding religious services and political conventions in a tree; but this Indian sham Quaker is just a rowdy, and is always noisy when awake—always chaffing, scolding, scoffing, laughing, ripping, and cursing, and carrying on about something or other. I never saw such a bird for delivering opinions. Nothing escapes him; he notices everything that happens, and brings out his opinion about it, particularly if it is a matter that is none of his business. And it is never a mild opinion, but always violent—violent and profane—the presence of ladies does not affect him. His opinions are not the outcome of reflection, for he never thinks about anything, but heaves out the opinion that is on top in his mind, and which is often an opinion about some quite different thing and does not fit the case. But that is his way; his main idea is to get out an opinion, and if he stopped to think he would lose chances.

I suppose he has no enemies among men. The whites and Mohammedans never seemed to molest him; and the Hindus, because of their religion, never take the life of any creature, but spare even the snakes and tigers and fleas and rats. If I sat on one end of the balcony, the crows would gather on the railing at the other end and talk about me; and edge closer, little by little, till I could almost reach them; and they would sit there, in the most unabashed way, and talk about my clothes, and my hair, and my complexion, and probable character and vocation and politics, and how I came to be in India, and what I had been doing, and how many days I had got for it, and how I had happened to go unhanged so long, and when would it probably come off, and might there be more of my sort where I came from, and when would *they* be hanged—and so on, and so on, until I could not longer endure the embarrassment of it; then I would shoo them away, and they would circle around in the air a little while, laughing and deriding and mocking, and presently settle on the rail and do it all over again.

They were very sociable when there was anything to eat—oppressively so. With a little encouragement they would come in and light on the table and help me eat my breakfast; and once when I was in the other room and they found themselves alone, they carried off everything they could lift; and they were particular to choose things which they could make no use of after they got them. In India their number is beyond estimate, and their noise is in proportion. I suppose they cost the country more than the government does; yet that is not a light matter. Still, they pay; their company pays; it would sadden the land to take their cheerful voice out of it.

INDIAN ELEPHANTS

By and by to the elephant stables, and I took a ride; but it was by request—I did not ask for it, and didn't want it; but I took it, because otherwise they would have thought I was afraid, which I was. The elephant kneels down, by command—one end of him at a time—and you climb the ladder and get into the howdah, and then he gets up, one end at a time, just as a ship gets up over a wave; and after that, as he strides monstrously about, his motion is much like a ship's motion. The mahout bores into the back of his head with a great iron prod, and you wonder at his temerity and at the elephant's patience, and you think that perhaps the patience will not last; but it does, and nothing happens. The mahout talks to the elephant in a low voice all the time, and the elephant seems to understand it all and to be pleased with it; and he obeys every order in the most contented and docile way. Among these twenty-five elephants were two which were larger than any I had ever seen before, and if I had thought I could learn to not be afraid, I would have taken one of them while the police were not looking.

In the howdah-house there were many howdahs that were made of silver, one of gold, and one of old ivory, and equipped with cushions and canopies of rich and costly stuffs. The wardrobe of the elephants was there, too; vast velvet covers stiff and heavy with gold embroidery; and bells of silver and gold; and ropes of these metals for fastening the things on—harness, so to speak; and monster hoops of massive gold for the elephant to wear on his ankles when he is out in procession on business of state.

THE IRON DOG

The drunken man reeled toward home late at night; made a mistake and entered the wrong gate; thought he saw a dog on the stoop; and it was—an iron one. He stopped and considered; wondered if it was a dangerous dog; ventured to say "Be (hic!) begone!" No effect. Then he approached warily, and adopted conciliation; pursed up his lips and tried to whistle, but failed; still approached, saying, "Poor dog!—doggy, doggy, doggy!—poor doggy-dog!" Got up on the stoop, still petting with fond names, till master of the advantages; then exclaimed, "Leave, you thief!"—planted a vindictive kick in his ribs, and went head-over-heels overboard, of course. A pause; a sigh or two of pain, and then a remark in a reflective voice:

"Awful solid dog. What could he b'en eating? ('ic!) Rocks, p'raps. Such animals is dangerous. 'At's what *I* say—they're dangerous. If a man—('ic!)—if a man wants to feed a dog on rocks, let him *feed* him on rocks; 'at's all right; but let him keep him at *home*—not have him layin' round promiscuous, where ('ic!) where people's liable to stumble over him when they ain't noticin'!"

J

THE JACKASS RABBIT

As the sun was going down, we saw the first specimen of an animal known familiarly over two thousand miles of mountain and desert—from Kansas clear to the Pacific Ocean—as the "jackass rabbit." He is well named. He is just like any other rabbit, except that he is from one-third to twice as large, has longer legs in proportion to his size, and has the most preposterous ears that ever were mounted on any creature *but* a jackass. When he is sitting quiet, thinking about his sins, or is absent-minded or unapprehensive of danger, his majestic ears project above him conspicuously; but the breaking of a twig will scare him nearly to death, and then he tilts his ears back gently and starts for home. All you can see, then, for the next minute, is his long gray form stretched out straight and "streaking it" through the low sage-brush, head erect, eyes right, and ears just canted a little to the rear, but showing you where the animal is, all the time, the same as if he carried a jib. Now and then he makes a marvelous spring with his long legs, high over the stunted sage-brush, and scores a leap that would make a horse envious. Presently, he comes down to a long, graceful "lope," and shortly he mysteriously disappears. He has crouched behind a sage-bush, and will sit there and listen and tremble until you get within six feet of him, when he will get under way again. But one must shoot at this creature once, if he wishes to see him throw his heart into his heels, and do the best he knows how. He is frightened clear through, now, and he lays his long ears down on his back, straightens himself out like a yardstick every spring he makes, and scatters miles behind him with an easy indifference that is enchanting.

Our party made this specimen "hump himself," as the conductor said. The Secretary started him with a shot from the Colt; I commenced spitting at him with my weapon; and all in the same instant the old "Allen's" whole broadside let go with a rattling crash, and it is not putting it too strong to say that the rabbit was frantic! He dropped his ears, set up his tail, and left for San Francisco at a speed which can only be described as a flash and a vanish! Long after he was out of sight we could hear him whiz.

JERICHO

While I am speaking of animals, I will mention that I have a horse now by the name of "Jericho." He is a mare. I have seen remarkable horses before, but none so remarkable as this. I wanted a horse that could shy, and this one fills the bill. I had an idea that shying indicated spirit. If I was correct, I have got the most spirited horse on earth. He shies at everything he comes across, with the utmost impartiality. He appears to have a mortal dread of telegraph-poles, especially; and it is fortunate that these are on both sides of the road, because as it is now, I never fall off twice in succession on the same side. If I fell on the same side always, it would get to be monotonous after a while. This creature has scared at everything he has seen today, except a haystack. He walked up to that with intrepidity and a recklessness that were astonishing. And it would fill any one with admiration to see how he preserves his self-possession in the presence of a barley sack. This dare devil bravery will be the death of this horse some day.

He is not particularly fast, but I think he will get me through the Holy Land. He has only one fault. His tail has been chopped off or else he has sat down on it too hard, some time or other, and he has to fight the flies with his heels. This is all very well, but when he tries to kick a fly off the top of his head with his hind foot, it is too much variety. He is going to get himself into trouble that way some day. He reaches around and bites my legs, too. I do not care particularly about that, only I do not like to see a horse too sociable.

I think the owner of this prize had a wrong opinion about him. He had an idea that he was one of those fiery, untamed steeds, but he is not of that character. I know the Arab had this idea, because when he brought the horse out for inspection in Beirout, he kept jerking at the bridle and shouting in Arabic, "Whoa! will you? Do you want to run away, you ferocious beast, and break your neck?" when all the time the horse was not doing anything in the world, and only looked like he wanted to lean up against something and think. Whenever he is not shying at things, or reaching after a fly, he wants to do that yet. How it would surprise his owner to know this.

JIM BAKER'S BLUEJAYS

Animals talk to each other, of course. There can be no question about that; but I suppose there are very few people who can understand them. I never knew but one man who could. I knew he could, however, because he told me so himself. He was a middle-aged, simple-hearted miner who had lived in a lonely corner of California, among the woods and mountains, a good many years, and had studied the ways of his only neighbors, the beasts and the birds, until he believed he could accurately translate any remark which they made. This was Jim Baker. According to Jim Baker, some animals have only a limited education, and use only very simple words, and scarcely ever a comparison or a flowery figure; whereas, certain other animals have a large vocabulary, a fine command of language and a ready and fluent delivery; consequently these latter talk a great deal; they like it; they are conscious of their talent, and they enjoy "show-

ing off." Baker said, that after long and careful observation, he had come to the conclusion that the bluejays were the best talkers he had found among birds and beasts. Said he:

"There's more *to* a bluejay than any other creature. He has got more moods, and more different kinds of feelings than other creatures; and, mind you, whatever a bluejay feels, he can put into language. And no mere commonplace language, either, but rattling, out-and-out booktalk—and bristling with metaphor, too—just bristling! And as for command of language—why *you* never see a bluejay get stuck for a word. No man ever did. They just boil out of him! And another thing: I've noticed a good deal, and there's no bird, or cow, or anything that uses as good grammar as a bluejay. You may say a cat uses good grammar. Well, a cat does—but you let a cat get excited once; you let a cat get to pulling fur with another cat on a shed, nights, and you'll hear grammar that will give you the lockjaw. Ignorant people think it's the *noise* which fighting cats make that is so aggravating, but it ain't so; it's the sickening grammar they use. Now I've never heard a jay use bad grammar but very seldom; and when they do, they are as ashamed as a human; they shut right down and leave.

"You may call a jay a bird. Well, so he is, in a measure—because he's got feathers on him, and don't belong to no church, perhaps; but otherwise he is just as much a human as you be. And I'll tell you for why. A jay's gifts, and instincts, and feelings, and interests, cover the whole ground. A jay hasn't got any more principle than a Congressman. A jay will lie, a jay will steal, a jay will deceive, a jay will betray; and four times out of five, a jay will go back on his solemnest promise. The sacredness of an obligation is a thing which you can't cram into no bluejay's head. Now, on top of all this, there's another thing; a jay can outswear any gentleman in the mines. You think a cat can swear. Well, a cat can; but you give a bluejay a subject that calls for his reserve-powers, and where is your cat? Don't talk to *me*—I know too much about this thing. And there's yet another thing; in the one little particular of scolding—just good, clean, out-and-out scolding—a bluejay can lay over anything, human or divine. Yes, sir, a jay is everything that a man is. A jay can cry, a jay can laugh, a jay can feel shame, a jay can reason and plan and discuss, a jay likes gossip and scandal, a jay has got a sense of humor, a jay knows when he is an ass just as well as you do—maybe better. If a jay ain't human, he better take in his sign, that's all. Now I'm going to tell you a perfectly true fact about some bluejays.

"When I first begun to understand jay language correctly, there was a little incident happened here. Seven years ago, the last man in this region but me moved away. There stands his house—been empty ever since; a log house, with a plank roof—just one big room, and no more; no ceiling—nothing between the rafters and the floor. Well, one Sunday morning I was sitting out here in front of my cabin, with my cat, taking the sun, and looking at the blue hills, and listening to the leaves rustling so lonely in the trees, and thinking of the home away yonder in the states, that I hadn't heard from in thirteen years, when a bluejay lit on that house, with an acorn in his mouth, and says, 'Hello, I reckon I've struck something.' When he spoke, the acorn dropped out of his mouth and rolled down the roof, of course, but he didn't care; his mind was all on the thing he had struck. It was a knot-hole in the roof. He cocked his head to one side, shut one eye and put the other one to the hole, like a possum looking down a jug; then he glanced up with his bright eyes, gave a wink or two with his wings—which signifies gratification, you understand—and says, 'It looks like a hole, it's located like a hole—blamed if I don't believe it *is* a hole!'

"Then he cocked his head down and took another look; he glances up perfectly joyful, this time; winks his wings and his tail both, and says, 'Oh, no, this ain't no fat thing, I reckon! If I ain't in luck!—why it's a perfectly elegant hole!' So he flew down and got that acorn, and fetched it up and dropped it in, and was just tilting his head back, with the heavenliest smile on his face, when all of a sudden he was paralyzed into a listening attitude and that smile faded gradually out of his countenance like breath off'n a razor, and the queerest look of surprise took its place. Then he says, 'Why, I didn't hear it fall!' He cocked his eye at the hole again, and took a long look; raised up and shook his head; stepped around to the other side of the hole and took another look from that side; shook his head again. He studied a while, then he just went into the *de*tails—walked round and round the hole and spied into it from every point of the compass. No use. Now he took a thinking attitude on the comb of the roof and scratched the back of his head with his right foot a minute, and finally says, 'Well, it's too many for *me*, that's certain; must be a mighty long hole; however, I

ain't got no time to fool around here, I got to 'tend to business; I reckon it's all right—chance it, anyway.'

"So he flew off and fetched another acorn and dropped it in, and tried to flirt his eye to the hole quick enough to see what become of it, but he was too late. He held his eye there as much as a minute; then he raised up and sighed, and says, 'Confound it, I don't seem to understand this thing, no way; however, I'll tackle her again.' He fetched another acorn, and done his level best to see what become of it, but he couldn't. He says, 'Well, *I* never struck no such a hole as this before; I'm of the opinion it's a totally new kind of a hole.' Then he begun to get mad. He held in for a spell, walking up and down the comb of the roof and shaking his head and muttering to himself; but his feelings got the upper hand of him, presently, and he broke loose and cussed himself black in the face. I never see a bird take on so about a little thing. When he got through he walks to the hole and looks in again for half a minute; then he says, 'Well, you're a long hole, and a deep hole, and a mighty singular hole altogether—but I've started in to fill you, and I'm d—d if I

don't fill you, if it takes a hundred years!'

"And with that, away he went. You never see a bird work so since you was born. He laid into his work . . . and the way he hove acorns into that hole for about two hours and a half was one of the most exciting and astonishing spectacles I ever struck. He never stopped to take a look any more—he just hove 'em in and went for more. Well, at last he could hardly flop his wings, he was so tuckered out. He comes a-dropping down, once more, sweating like an ice-pitcher, drops his acorn in and says, '*Now* I guess I've got the bulge on you by this time!' So he bent down for a look. If you'll believe me, when his head come up again he was just pale with rage. He says, 'I've shoveled acorns enough in there to keep the family thirty years, and if I can see a sign of one of 'em I wish I may land in a museum with a belly full of sawdust in two minutes!'

"He just had strength enough to crawl up on to the comb and lean his back agin the chimbly, and then he collected his impressions and begun to free his mind. I see in a second that what I had mistook for profanity in the mines was only just the rudiments, as you may say.

"Another jay was going by, and heard him doing his devotions, and stops to inquire what was up. The sufferer told him the whole circumstance, and says, 'Now yonder's the hole, and if you don't believe me, go and look for yourself.' So this fellow went and looked, and comes back and says, 'How many did you say you put in there?' 'Not any less than two tons,' says the sufferer. The other jay went and looked again. He couldn't seem to make it out, so he raised a yell, and three more jays come. They all examined the hole, they all made the sufferer tell it over again, they they all discussed it, and got off as many leather-headed opinions about it as an average crowd of humans could have done.

"They called in more jays; then more and more, till pretty soon this whole region 'peared to have a blue flush about it. There must have been five thousand of them; and such another jawing and disputing and ripping and cussing, you never heard. Every jay in the whole lot put his eye to the hole and delivered a more chuckle-headed opinion about the mystery than the jay that went there before him. They examined the house all over, too. The door was standing half open, and at last one old jay happened to go and light on it and look in. Of course, that knocked the mystery galley-west in a second. There lay the acorns, scattered all over the floor. He flopped his wings and raised a whoop. 'Come here!' he says, 'Come here, everybody; hang'd if this fool hasn't been trying to fill up a house with acorns!' They all came a-swooping down like a blue cloud, and as each fellow lit on the door and took a glance, the whole absurdity of the contract that first jay had tackled hit him home and he fell over backward suffocating with laughter, and the next jay took his place and done the same.

"Well, sir, they roosted around here on the housetop and the trees for an hour, and guffawed over that thing like human beings. It ain't any use to tell me a bluejay hasn't got a sense of humor, because I know better. And memory, too. They brought jays here from all over the United States to look down that hole, every summer for three years. Other birds, too. And they could all see the point, except an owl that come from Nova Scotia to visit the Yo Semite, and he took this thing in on his way back. He said he couldn't see anything funny in it. But then he was a good deal disappointed about Yo Semite, too."

JIM WOLF AND THE WASPS

It may be that Jim Wolf was as bashful as [Joel Chandler] Harris. It hardly seems possible, yet as I look back fifty-six years and consider Jim Wolf, I am almost persuaded that he was. He was our long slim apprentice in my brother's printing office in Hannibal. . . . (However, in an earlier chapter I have already introduced him.

He was the lad whom I assisted with uninvited advice and sympathy the night he had the memorable adventure with the cats.) He was seventeen and yet he was as much as four times as bashful as I was, though I was only fourteen. He boarded and slept in the house but he was always tongue-tied in the presence of my sister, and when even my gentle mother spoke to him he could not answer save in frightened monosyllables. He would not enter a room where a girl was; nothing could persuade him to do such a thing.

Once when he was in our small parlor alone, two majestic old maids entered and seated themselves in such a way that Jim could not escape without passing by them. He would as soon have thought of passing by one of Harris's plesiosaurians, ninety feet long. I came in presently, was charmed with the situation, and sat down in a corner to watch Jim suffer and to enjoy it. My mother followed, a minute later, and sat down with the visitors and began to talk. Jim sat upright in his chair and during a quarter of an hour he did not change his position by a shade—neither General Grant nor a bronze image could have maintained that immovable pose more successfully. I mean as to body and limbs; with the face there was a difference. By fleeting revealments of the face I saw that something was happening—something out of the common. There would be a sudden twitch of the muscles of the face, an instant distortion which in the next instant had passed and left no trace. These twitches gradually grew in frequency but no muscle outside of the face lost any of its rigidity, or betrayed any interest in what was happening to Jim. I mean if something *was* happening to him, and I knew perfectly well that that was the case. At last a pair of tears began to swim slowly down his cheeks amongst the twitchings, but Jim sat still and let them run; then I saw his right hand steal along his thigh until halfway to his knee, then take a vigorous grip upon the cloth.

That was a wasp that he was grabbing. A colony of them were climbing up his legs and prospecting around, and every time he winced they stabbed him to the hilt— so for a quarter of an hour one group of excursionists after another climbed up Jim's legs and resented even the slightest wince or squirm that he indulged himself with in his misery. When the entertainment had become nearly unbearable, he conceived the idea of gripping them between his fingers and putting them out of commission. He succeeded with many of them but at great cost, for as he couldn't see the wasp he was as likely to take hold of the wrong end of him as he was the right; then the dying wasp gave him a punch to remember the incident by.

If those ladies had stayed all day and if all the wasps in

Missouri had come and climbed up Jim's legs, nobody there would ever have known it but Jim and the wasps and me. There he would have sat until the ladies left. When they were gone we went upstairs and he took his clothes off, and his legs were a picture to look at. They looked as if they were mailed all over with shirt buttons, each with a single red hole in the center. The pain was intolerable—no, would have been intolerable, but the pain of the presence of those ladies had been so much harder to bear that the pain of the wasps' stings was quite pleasant and enjoyable by comparison.

Jim never could enjoy wasps. I remember once——

JOAN OF ARC'S DRAGON

Our Domremy was like any other humble little hamlet of that remote time and region. It was a maze of crooked, narrow lanes and alleys shaded and sheltered by the over-hanging thatch roofs of the barnlike houses. The houses were dimly lighted by wooden-shuttered windows—that is, holes in the walls which served for windows. The floors were of dirt, and there was very little furniture. Sheep and cattle grazing was the main industry; all the young folks tended flocks.

The situation was beautiful. From one edge of the village a flowery plain extended in a wide sweep to the river—the Meuse; from the rear edge of the village a grassy slope rose gradually, and at the top was the great oak forest—a forest that was deep and gloomy and dense, and full of interest for us children, for many murders had been done in it by outlaws in old times, and in still earlier times prodigious dragons that spouted fire and poisonous vapors from their nostrils had their homes in there. In fact, one was still living in there in our own time. It was as long as a tree, and had a body as big around as a tierce, and scales like overlapping great tiles, and deep ruby eyes as large as a cavalier's hat, and an anchor-fluke on its tail as big as I don't know what, but very big, even unusually so for a dragon, as everybody said who knew about dragons. It was thought that this dragon was of a brilliant blue color, with gold mottlings, but no one had ever seen it, therefore this was not known to be so, it was only an opinion. It was not my opinion; I think there is no sense in forming an opinion when there is no evidence to form it on. If you build a person with-out any bones in him he may look fair enough to the eye, but he will be limber and cannot stand up; and I consider that *evidence* is the bones of an opinion. But I will take up this matter more at large at another time, and try to make the justness of my position appear. As to that dragon, I always held the belief that its color was gold and without blue, for that has always been the color of dragons. That this dragon lay but a little way within the wood at one time is shown by the fact that Pierre Morel was in there one day and smelt it, and recognized it by the smell. It gives one a horrid idea of how near to us the deadliest danger can be and .we not suspect it.

K

THE KITTEN IN THE CORNER-POCKET

REDDING, CONNECTICUT,
Oct. 2, 08.

DEAR MRS. PATTERSON,—The contents of your letter are very pleasant and very welcome, and I thank you for them, sincerely. If I can find a photograph of my "Tammany" and her kittens, I will enclose it in this. One of them likes to be crammed into a corner-pocket of the billiard table—which he fits as snugly as does a finger in a glove and then he watches the game (and obstructs it) by the hour, and spoils many a shot by putting out his paw and changing the direction of a passing ball. Whenever a ball is in his arms, or so close to him that it cannot be played upon without risk of hurting him, the player is privileged to remove it to anyone of the 3 spots that chances to be vacant. . . .

Sincerely yours,
S. L. CLEMENS.

L

THE LAUGHING JACKASS

In the Zoological Gardens of Adelaide I saw the only laughing jackass that ever showed any disposition to be courteous to me. This one opened his head wide and laughed like a demon; or like a maniac who was consumed with humorous scorn over a cheap and degraded pun. It was a very human laugh. If he had been out of sight I could have believed that the laughter came from a man. It is an odd-looking bird, with a head and beak that are much too large for its body. In time man will exterminate the rest of the wild creatures of Australia, but this one will probably survive, for man is his friend and lets him alone. Man always has a good reason for his charities toward wild things, human or animal—when he has any. In this case the bird is spared because he kills snakes. If L.J. will take my advice he will not kill all of them.

THE LIGNIFIED CATERPILLAR

Dr. Hockin gave us a ghastly curiosity—a lignified caterpillar with a plant growing out of the back of its neck—a plant with a slender stem four inches high. It happened not by accident, but by design—Nature's design. This caterpillar was in the act of loyally carrying out a law inflicted upon him by Nature—a law purposely inflicted upon him to get him into trouble—a law which was a trap; in pursuance of this law he made the proper preparations for turning himself into a night-moth; that is to say, he dug a little trench, a little grave, and then stretched himself out in it on his stomach and partially buried himself—then Nature was ready for him. She blew the spores of a peculiar fungus through the air—with a purpose. Some of them fell into a crease in the back of the caterpillar's neck, and began to sprout and grow—for there was soil there—he had not washed his neck. The roots forced themselves down into the worm's person, and rearward along through its body, sucking up the creature's juices for sap; the worm slowly died, and turned to wood. And here he was now, a wooden caterpillar, with every detail of his former physique delicately and exactly preserved and perpetuated, and with that stem standing up out of him for his monument—monument commemorative of his own loyalty and of Nature's unfair return for it.

A LONG-LEGGED BIRD

In the great Zoological Gardens we found specimens of all the animals the world produces, I think, including a dromedary, a monkey ornamented with tufts of brilliant blue and carmine hair—a very gorgeous monkey he was—a hippopotamus from the Nile, and a sort of tall, long-legged bird with a beak like a powder-horn, and close-fitting wings like the tails of a dress-coat. This fellow stood up with his eyes shut and his shoulders

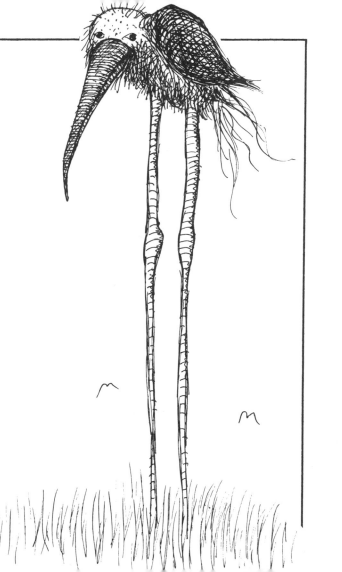

stooped forward a little, and looked as if he had his hands under his coat-tails. Such tranquil stupidity, such supernatural gravity, such self-righteousness, and such ineffable self-complacency as were in the countenance and attitude of that gray-bodied, dark-winged, bald-headed, and preposterously uncomely bird! He was so ungainly, so pimply about the head, so scaly about the legs; yet so serene, so unspeakably satisfied! He was the most comical-looking creature that can be imagined. It was good to hear Dan and the doctor laugh—such natural and such enjoyable laughter had not been heard among our excursionists since our ship sailed away from America. This bird was a godsend to us, and I should be an ingrate if I forgot to make honorable mention of him in these pages. Ours was a pleasure excursion; therefore we stayed with that bird an hour, and made the most of him. We stirred him up occasionally, but he only unclosed an eye and slowly closed it again, abating no jot of his stately piety of demeanor or his tremendous seriousness. He only seemed to say, "Defile not Heaven's anointed with unsanctified hands." We did not know his name, and so we called him "The Pilgrim."

M

THE MOA

The Moa stood thirteen feet high, and could step over an ordinary man's head or kick his hat off; and his head, too, for that matter. He said it was wingless, but a swift runner. The natives used to ride it. It could make forty miles an hour, and keep it up for four hundred miles and come out reasonably fresh. It was still in existence when the railway was introduced into New Zealand; still in existence and carrying the mails. The railroad began with the same schedule it has now: two expresses a week—time, twenty miles an hour. The company exterminated the Moa to get the mails.

THE MONKEY
OF THE MINARETS

The most conspicuous feature of Benares is the pair of slender white minarets which tower like masts from the great Mosque of Aurangzeb. They seem to be always in sight, from everywhere, those airy, graceful, inspiring things. But masts is not the right word, for masts have a perceptible taper, while these minarets have not. They are 142 feet high, and only 8½ feet in diameter at the base, and 7½ at the summit—scarcely any taper at all. These are the proportions of a candle; and fair and fairylike candles these are. Will be, anyway, some day, when the Christians inherit them and top them with the electric light. There is a great view from up there—a wonderful view. A large gray monkey was part of it, and damaged it. A monkey has no judgment. This one was skipping about the upper great heights of the mosque— skipping across empty yawning intervals which were almost too wide for him, and which he only just barely cleared, each time, by the skin of his teeth. He got me so nervous that I couldn't look at the view. I couldn't look at anything but him. Every time he went sailing over one of those abysses my breath stood still, and when he grabbed for the perch he was going for, I grabbed too, in sympathy. And he was perfectly indifferent, perfectly unconcerned, and I did all the panting myself. He came within an ace of losing his life a dozen times, and I was so troubled about him that I would have shot him if I had had anything to do it with. But I strongly recommend the view. There is more monkey than view, and there is always going to be more monkey while that idiot survives, but what view you get is superb. All Benares, the river, and the region round about are spread before you. Take a gun, and look at the view.

MOSQUITOES

Stack Island. I remembered Stack Island; also Lake Providence, Louisiana—which is the first distinctly Southern-looking town you come to, downward bound; lies level and low, shade-trees hung with venerable gray-beards of Spanish moss; "restful, pensive, Sunday aspect about the place," comments Uncle Mumford, with feeling—also with truth.

A Mr. H. furnished some minor details of fact concerning this region which I would have hesitated to believe, if I had not known him to be a steamboat mate. He was a passenger of ours, a resident of Arkansas City, and bound to Vicksburg to join his boat, a little Sunflower packet. He was an austere man, and had the reputation of being singularly unworldly, for a river-man. Among other things, he said that Arkansas had been injured and kept back by generations of exaggerations concerning the mosquitoes there. One may smile, said he, and turn the matter off as being a small thing; but when you come to look at the effects produced, in the way of discouragement of immigration and diminished values of property, it was quite the opposite of a small thing, or thing in any wise to be coughed down or sneered at. These mosquitoes had been persistently represented as being formidable and lawless; whereas "the truth is, they are feeble, insignificant in size, diffident to a fault, sensitive"—and so on, and so on; you would have supposed he was talking about his family. But if he was soft on the Arkansas mosquitoes, he was hard enough on the mosquitoes of Lake Providence to make up for it—"those Lake Providence colossi," as he finely called them. He said that two of them could whip a dog, and that four of them could hold a man down; and except help come, they would kill him—"butcher him," as he expressed it. Referred in a sort of casual way—and yet significant way, to "the fact that the life policy in its simplest form is unknown in Lake Providence—they take out a mosquito policy besides." He told many remarkable things about those lawless insects. Among others, said he had seen them try to *vote*. Noticing that this statement seemed to be a good deal of a strain on us, he modified it a little; said he might have been mistaken as to that particular, but knew he had seen them around the polls "canvassing."

MOUNTAIN-CLIMBING MULES

We met an everlasting procession of guides, porters, mules, litters, and tourists climbing up this steep and muddy path, and there was no room to spare when you had to pass a tolerably fat mule. I always took the inside, when I heard or saw the mule coming, and flattened myself against the wall. I preferred the inside, of course, but I should have had to take it anyhow, because the mule prefers the outside. A mule's preference—on a precipice—is a thing to be respected. Well, his choice is always the outside. His life is mostly devoted to carrying bulky panniers and packages which rest against his body—therefore he is habituated to taking the outside edge of mountain paths, to keep his bundles from rubbing against rocks or banks on the other. When he goes into the passenger business he absurdly clings to his old habit, and keeps one leg of his passenger always dangling over the great deeps of the lower world while that passenger's heart is in the highlands, so to speak. More than once I saw a mule's hind foot cave over the outer edge and send earth and rubbish into the bottomless abyss; and I noticed that upon these occasions the rider, whether male or female, looked tolerably unwell.

There was one place where an eighteen-inch breadth of light masonry had been added to the verge of the path, and as there was a very sharp turn here, a panel of fencing had been set up there at some ancient time, as a protection. This panel was old and gray and feeble, and the light masonry had been loosened by recent rains. A young American girl came along on a mule, and in making the turn the mule's hind foot caved all the loose masonry and one of the fence-posts overboard; the mule gave a violent lurch inboard to save himself, and succeeded in the effort, but that girl turned as white as the snows of Mont Blanc for a moment.

The path here was simply a groove cut into the face of the precipice; there was a four-foot breadth of solid rock under the traveler, and a four-foot breadth of solid rock just above his head, like the roof of a narrow porch; he could look out from this gallery and see a sheer summitless and bottomless wall of rock before him, across a gorge or a crack, a biscuit's toss in width—but he could not see the bottom of his own precipice unless he lay down and projected his nose over the edge. I did not do this, because I did not wish to soil my clothes.

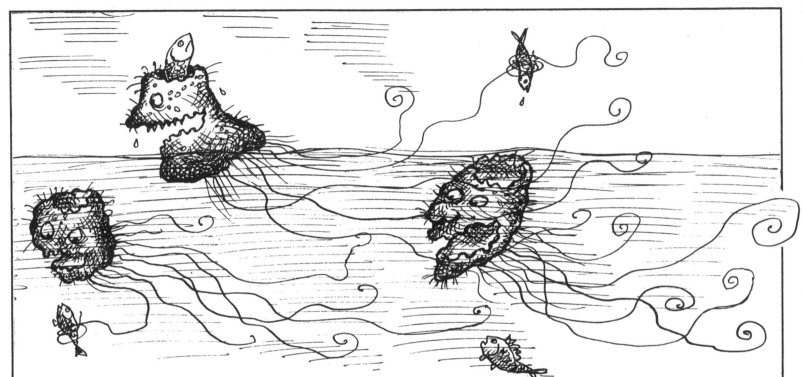

THE NAUTILUS

The nautilus is nothing but a transparent web of jelly, that spreads itself to catch the wind, and has fleshy-looking strings a foot or two long dangling from it to keep it steady in the water. It is an accomplished sailor, and has good sailor judgment. It reefs its sail when a storm threatens or the wind blows pretty hard, and furls it entirely and goes down when a gale blows. Ordinarily it keeps its sail wet and in good sailing order by turning over and dipping it in the water for a moment.

NOISE-MAKING BIRDS

Half-way down the mountain we stopped about an hour at Mr. Barnard's house for refreshments, and while we were sitting on the veranda looking at the distant panorama of hills through a gap in the forest, we came very near seeing a leopard kill a calf.[1] It is a wild place and lovely. From the woods all about came the songs of birds—among them the contributions of a couple of birds which I was not then acquainted with: the brain-fever bird and the coppersmith. The song of the brain-fever demon starts on a low but steadily rising key, and is a spiral twist which augments in intensity and severity with each added spiral, growing sharper and sharper, and more and more painful, more and more agonizing, more and more maddening, intolerable, unendurable, as it bores deeper and deeper and deeper into the listener's brain, until at last the brain-fever comes as a relief and the man dies. I am bringing some of these birds home to America. They will be a great curiosity there, and it is believed that in our climate they will multiply like rabbits.

The coppersmith bird's note at a certain distance away has the ring of a sledge on granite; at a certain other distance the hammering has a more metallic ring, and you might think that the bird was mending a copper

[1]It killed it the day before.—*M.T.*

kettle; at another distance it has a more woodeny thump, but it is a thump that is full of energy, and sounds just like starting a bung. So he is a hard bird to name with a single name; he is a stone-breaker, coppersmith, and bung-starter, and even then he is not completely named, for when he is close by you find that there is a soft, deep, melodious quality in his thump, and for that no satisfying name occurs to you. You will not mind his other notes, but when he camps near enough for you to hear that one, you presently find that his measured and monotonous repetition of it is beginning to disturb you; next it will weary you, soon it will distress you, and before long each thump will hurt your head; if this goes on, you will lose your mind with the pain and misery of it, and go crazy. I am bringing some of these birds home to America. There is nothing like them there. They will be a great surprise, and it is said that in a climate like ours they will surpass expectation for fecundity.

I am bringing some nightingales, too, and some cue-owls. I got them in Italy. The song of the nightingale is the deadliest known to ornithology. That demoniacal shriek can kill at thirty yards. The note of the cue-owl is infinitely soft and sweet—soft and sweet as the whisper of a flute. But penetrating—oh, beyond belief; it can bore through boiler-iron. It is a lingering note, and comes in triplets, on the one unchanging key: *hoo-o-o, hoo-o-o,* *hoo-o-o*; then a silence of fifteen seconds, then the triplet again; and so on, all night. At first it is divine; then less so; then trying; then distressing; then excruciating; then agonizing, and at the end of two hours the listener is a maniac.

0

OAHU

The landlord of the American said the party had been gone nearly an hour, but that he could give me my choice of several horses that could overtake them. I said, never mind—I preferred a safe horse to a fast one—I would like to have an excessively gentle horse—a horse with no spirit whatever—a lame one, if he had such a thing. Inside of five minutes I was mounted, and perfectly satisfied with my outfit. I had no time to label him "This is a horse," and so if the public took him for a sheep I cannot help it. I was satisfied, and that was the main thing. I could see that he had as many fine points as any man's horse, and so I hung my hat on one of them, behind the saddle, and swabbed the perspiration from my face and started. I named him after this island, "Oahu" (pronounced O-waw-hee). The first gate he came to he started in; I had neither whip nor spur, and so I simply argued the case with him. He resisted argument, but ultimately yielded to insult and abuse. He backed out of that gate and steered for another one on the other side of the street. I triumphed by my former process. Within the next six hundred yards he crossed the street fourteen times and attempted thirteen gates, and in the mean time the tropical sun was beating down and threatening to cave the top of my head in, and I was literally dripping with perspiration. He abandoned the gate business after that and went along peaceably enough, but absorbed in meditation. I noticed this latter circumstance, and it soon began to fill me with apprehension. I said to myself, this creature is planning some new outrage, some fresh deviltry or other—no horse ever thought over a subject so profoundly as this one is doing just for nothing. The more this thing preyed upon my mind the more uneasy I became, until the suspense became almost unbearable, and I dismounted to see if there was anything wild in his eye—for I had heard that the eye of this noblest of our domestic animals is very expressive. I cannot describe what a load of anxiety was lifted from my mind when I found that he was only asleep. I woke him up and started him into a faster walk, and then the villainy of his nature came out again. He tried to climb over a stone wall, five or six feet high. I saw that I must apply force to this horse, and that I might as well begin first as last. I plucked a stout switch from a tamarind tree, and the moment he saw it, he surrendered. He broke into a convulsive sort of a canter, which had three short steps in it and one long one, and reminded me alternately of the clattering shake of the great earthquake, and the sweeping plunge of the *Ajax* in a storm.

THE ORNITHORHYNCUS

Speaking of the indigenous coneys and bactrian camels, the naturalist said that the coniferous and bacteriological output of Australasia was remarkable for its many and curious departures from the accepted laws governing these species of tubercles, but that in his opinion Nature's fondness for dabbling in the erratic was most notably exhibited in that curious combination of bird, fish, amphibian, burrower, crawler, quadruped, and Christian called the Ornithorhyncus—grotesquest of animals, king of the animalculae of the world for versatility of character and make-up. Said he:

You can call it anything you want to, and be right. It is a fish, for it lives in the river half the time; it is a land-animal, for it resides on the land half the time; it is an amphibian, since it likes both and does not know which it prefers; it is a hybernian, for when times are dull and nothing much going on it buries itself under the mud at the bottom of a puddle and hybernates there a couple of weeks at a time; it is a kind of duck, for it has a duck-bill and four webbed paddles; it is a fish and quadruped together, for in the water it swims with the paddles and on shore it paws itself across country with them; it is

a kind of seal, for it has a seal's fur; it is carnivorous, herbivorous, insectivorous, and vermifuginous, for it eats fish and grass and butterflies, and in the season digs worms out of the mud and devours them; it is clearly a bird, for it lays eggs and hatches them; it is clearly a mammal, for it nurses its young; and it is manifestly a kind of Christian, for it keeps the Sabbath when there is anybody around, and when there isn't, doesn't. It has all the tastes there are except refined ones, it has all the habits there are except good ones.

It is a survival—a survival of the fittest. Mr. Darwin invented the theory that goes by that name, but the Ornithorhyncus was the first to put it to actual experiment and prove that it could be done. Hence it should have as much of the credit as Mr. Darwin. It was never in the Ark; you will find no mention of it there; it nobly stayed out and worked the theory. Of all creatures in the world it was the only one properly equipped for the test. The Ark was thirteen months afloat, and all the globe submerged; no land visible above the flood, no vegetation, no food for a mammal to eat, nor water for a mammal to drink; for all mammal food was destroyed, and when the pure floods from heaven and the salt oceans of the earth mingled their waters and rose above the mountain-tops, the result was a drink which no bird or beast of ordinary construction could use and live. But this combination was nuts for the Ornithorhyncus, if I may use a term like that without offense. Its river home had always been salted by the flood-tides of the sea. On the face of the Noachian deluge innumerable forest trees were floating. Upon these the Ornithorhyncus voyaged in peace; voyaged from clime to clime, from hemisphere to hemisphere, in contentment and comfort, in virile interest in the constant change of scene, in humble thankfulness for its privileges, in ever-increasing enthusiasm in the development of the great theory upon whose validity it had staked its life, its fortunes, and its sacred honor, if I may use such expressions without impropriety in connection with an episode of this nature.

It lived the tranquil and luxurious life of a creature of independent means. Of things actually necessary to its existence and its happiness not a detail was wanting. When it wished to walk, it scrambled along the tree-trunk; it mused in the shade of the leaves by day, it slept in their shelter by night; when it wanted the refreshment of a swim, it had it; it ate leaves when it wanted a vegetable diet, it dug under the bark for worms and grubs; when it wanted fish it caught them, when it wanted eggs it laid them. If the grubs gave out in one tree it swam to another; and as for fish, the very opulence of the supply was an embarrassment. And finally, when it was thirsty it smacked its chops in gratitude over a blend that would have slain a crocodile.

When at last, after thirteen months of travel and research in all the Zones, it went aground on a mountain-summit, it strode ashore, saying in its heart, "Let them that come after me invent theories and dream dreams about the Survival of the Fittest if they like, but I am the first that has *done* it!"

This wonderful creature dates back, like the kangaroo and many other Australian hydrocephalous invertebrates, to an age long anterior to the advent of man upon the earth; they date back, indeed, to a time when a causeway, hundreds of miles wide and thousands of miles long, joined Australia to Africa, and the animals of the two countries were alike, and all belonged to that remote geological epoch known to science as the Old Red Grindstone Post-Pleosaurian. Later the causeway sank under the sea; subterranean convulsions lifted the African continent a thousand feet higher than it was before, but Australia kept her old level. In Africa's new climate the animals necessarily began to develop and shade off into new forms and families and species, but the animals of Australia as necessarily remained stationary, and have so remained until this day. In the course of some millions of years the African Ornithorhyncus developed and developed and developed, and sloughed off detail after detail of its make-up until at last the creature became wholly disintegrated and scattered. Whenever you see a bird or a beast or a seal or an otter in Africa you know that he is merely a sorry surviving fragment of that sublime original of whom I have been speaking—that creature which was everything in general and nothing in particular—the opulently endowed *e pluribus unum* of the animal world.

Such is the history of the most hoary, the most ancient, the most venerable creature that exists in the earth to-day—*Ornithorhyncus Platypus Extraordinariensis*—whom God preserve!

P

THE PINCHBUG AND
THE POODLE

The minister made a grand and moving picture of the assembling together of the world's hosts at the millennium when the lion and the lamb should lie down together and a little child should lead them. But the pathos, the lesson, the moral of the great spectacle were lost upon the boy; he only thought of the conspicuousness of the principal character before the onlooking nations; his face lit with the thought, and he said to himself that he wished he could be that child, if it was a tame lion.

Now he lapsed into suffering again, as the dry argument was resumed. Presently he bethought him of a treasure he had and got it out. It was a large black beetle with formidable jaws—a "pinchbug," he called it. It was in a percussion-cap box. The first thing the beetle did was to take him by the finger. A natural fillip followed, the beetle went floundering into the aisle and lit on its back, and the hurt finger went into the boy's mouth. The beetle lay there working its helpless legs, unable to turn over. Tom eyed it, and longed for it; but it was safe out of his reach. Other people uninterested in the sermon, found relief in the beetle, and they eyed it too. Presently a vagrant poodle-dog came idling along, sad at heart, lazy with the summer softness and the quiet, weary of captivity, sighing for change. He spied the beetle; the drooping tail lifted and wagged. He surveyed the prize; walked around it; smelt at it from a safe distance; walked around it again; grew bolder, and took a closer smell; then lifted his lip and made a gingerly snatch at it, just missing it; made another, and another; began to enjoy the diversion; subsided to his stomach with the beetle between his paws, and continued his experiments; grew weary at last, and then indifferent and absent-minded. His head nodded, and little by little his chin descended and touched the enemy, who seized it. There was a sharp yelp, a flirt of the poodle's head, and the beetle fell a couple of yards away, and lit on its back once more. The neighboring spectators shook with a gentle inward joy, several faces went behind fans and handkerchiefs, and Tom was entirely happy. The dog looked foolish, and probably felt so; but there was resentment in his heart, too, and a craving for revenge. So he went to the beetle and began a wary attack on it again; jumping at it from every point of a circle, lighting with his fore paws within an inch of the creature, making even closer snatches at it with his teeth, and jerking his head till his ears flapped again. But he grew tired once more, after a while; tried

to amuse himself with a fly but found no relief; followed an ant around, with his nose close to the floor, and quickly wearied of that; yawned, sighed, forgot the beetle entirely, and sat down on it. Then there was a wild yelp of agony and the poodle went sailing up the aisle; the yelps continued, and so did the dog; he crossed the house in front of the altar; he flew down the other aisle; he crossed before the doors; he clamored up the home-stretch; his anguish grew with his progress, till presently he was but a woolly comet moving in its orbit with the gleam and the speed of light. At last the frantic sufferer sheered from its course, and sprang into its master's lap; he flung it out of the window, and the voice of distress quickly thinned away and died in the distance.

By this time the whole church was red-faced and suffocating with suppressed laughter, and the sermon had come to a dead standstill.

A PLAGUE OF RABBITS

In New Zealand the rabbit plague began at Bluff. The man who introduced the rabbit there was banqueted and lauded; but they would hang him, now, if they could get him. In England the natural enemy of the rabbit is detested and persecuted; in the Bluff region the natural enemy of the rabbit is honored, and his person is sacred. The rabbit's natural enemy in England is the poacher; in Bluff its natural enemy is the stoat, the weasel, the ferret, the cat, and the mongoose. In England any person below the Heir who is caught with a rabbit in his possession must satisfactorily explain how it got there, or he will suffer fine and imprisonment, together with extinction of his peerage; in Bluff, the cat found with a rabbit in its possession does not have to explain—everybody looks the other way; the person caught noticing would suffer fine and imprisonment, with extinction of peerage. This is a

sure way to undermine the moral fabric of a cat. Thirty years from now there will not be a moral cat in New Zealand. Some think there is none there now. In England the poacher is watched, tracked, hunted—he dare not show his face; in Bluff the cat, the weasel, the stoat, and the mongoose go up and down, whither they will, unmolested. By a law of the legislature, posted where all may read, it is decreed that any person found in possession of one of these creatures (dead) must satisfactorily explain the circumstances or pay a fine of not less than five pounds, nor more than twenty pounds. The revenue from this source is not large. Persons who want to pay a hundred dollars for a dead cat are getting rarer and rarer every day. This is bad, for the revenue was to go to the endowment of a university. All governments are more or less short-sighted: in England they fine a poacher, whereas he ought to be banished to New Zealand. New Zealand would pay his way, and give him wages.

PORPOISES

Sept. 15–Night. Close to Australia now. Sydney fifty miles distant.

That note recalls an experience. The passengers were sent for, to come up in the bow and see a fine sight. It was very dark. One could not follow with the eye the surface of the sea more than fifty yards in any direction—it dimmed away and became lost to sight at about that distance from us. But if you patiently gazed into the darkness a little while, there was a sure reward for you. Presently, a quarter of a mile away you would see a blinding splash or explosion of light on the water—a flash so sudden and so astonishingly brilliant that it would make you catch your breath; then that blotch of light would instantly extend itself and take the corkscrew shape and imposing length of the fabled sea-serpent, with every curve of its body and the "break" spreading away from its head, and the wake following behind its tail clothed in a fierce splendor of living fire. And my, but it was coming at a lightning gait! Almost before you could think, this monster of light, fifty feet long, would go flaming and storming by, and suddenly disappear. And out in the distance whence he came you would see another flash; and another and another and another, and see them turn into sea-serpents on the instant; and once sixteen flashed up at the same time and came tearing toward us, a swarm of wiggling curves, a moving conflagration, a vision of bewildering beauty, a spectacle of fire and energy whose equal the most of those people will not see again until after they are dead.

It was porpoises—porpoises aglow with phosphorescent light. They presently collected in a wild and magnificent jumble under the bows, and there they played for an hour, leaping and frolicking and carrying on, turning somersaults in front of the stem or across it and never getting hit, never making a miscalculation, though the stem missed them only about an inch, as a rule. They were porpoises of the ordinary length—eight or ten feet—but every twist of their bodies sent a long procession of united and glowing curves astern. That fiery jumble was an enchanting thing to look at, and we stayed out the performance; one cannot have such a show as that twice in a lifetime. The porpoise is the kitten of the sea; he never has a serious thought, he cares for nothing but fun and play. But I think I never saw him at his winsomest until that night. It was near a center of civilization, and he could have been drinking.

108

THE QUEEN BEE

Bee scientists always speak of the bee as she. It is because all the important bees are of that sex. In the hive there is one married bee, called the queen; she has fifty thousand children; of these, about one hundred are sons; the rest are daughters. Some of the daughters are young maids, some are old maids, and all are virgins and remain so.

Every spring the queen comes out of the hive and flies away with one of her sons and marries him. The honeymoon lasts only an hour or two; then the queen divorces

her husband and returns home competent to lay two million eggs. This will be enough to last the year, but not more than enough, because hundreds of bees get drowned every day, and other hundreds are eaten by birds, and it is the queen's business to keep the population up to standard—say, fifty thousand. She must always have that many children on hand and efficient during the busy season, which is summer, or winter would catch the community short of food. She lays from two thousand to three thousand eggs a day, according to the demand; and she must exercise judgment, and not lay more than are needed in a slim flower-harvest, nor fewer than are required in a prodigal one, or the board of directors will dethrone her and elect a queen that has more sense.

There are always a few royal heirs in stock and ready to take her place—ready and more than anxious to do it, although she is their own mother. These girls are kept by themselves, and are regally fed and tended from birth. No other bees get such fine food as they get, or live such a high and luxurious life. By consequence they are larger and longer and sleeker than their working sisters. And they have a curved sting, shaped like a simitar, while the others have a straight one. . . .

During substantially the whole of her short life of five or six years the queen lives in the Egyptian darkness and stately seclusion of the royal apartments, with none about

her but plebeian servants, who give her empty lip-affection in place of the love which her heart hungers for; who spy upon her in the interest of her waiting heirs, and report and exaggerate her defects and deficiencies to them; who fawn upon her and flatter her to her face and slander her behind her back; who grovel before her in the day of her power and forsake her in her age and weakness. There she sits, friendless, upon her throne through the long night of her life, cut off from the consoling sympathies and sweet companionship and loving endearments which she craves, by the gilded barriers of her awful rank; a forlorn exile in her own house and home, weary object of formal ceremonies and machine-made worship, winged child of the sun, native to the free air and the blue skies and the flowery fields, doomed by the splendid accident of her birth to trade this priceless heritage for a black captivity, a tinsel grandeur, and a loveless life, with shame and insult at the end and a cruel death—and condemned by the human instinct in her to hold the bargain valuable!

R

RACING MULES

We assisted—in the French sense—at a mule-race, one day. I believe I enjoyed this contest more than any other mule there. I enjoyed it more than I remember having enjoyed any other animal race I ever saw. The grandstand was well filled with the beauty and the chivalry of New Orleans. That phrase is not original with me. It is the Southern reporter's. He has used it for two generations. He uses it twenty times a day, or twenty thousand times a day, or a million times a day—according to the exigencies. He is obliged to use it a million times a day, if he have occasion to speak of respectable men and women that often; for he has no other phrase for such service except that single one. . . .

There were thirteen mules in the first heat; all sorts of mules, they were; all sorts of complexions, gaits, dispositions, aspects. Some were handsome creatures, some were not; some were sleek, some hadn't had their fur brushed lately; some were innocently gay and frisky; some were full of malice and all unrighteousness; guessing from looks, some of them thought the matter on hand was war, some thought it was a lark, the rest took it for a religious occasion. And each mule acted according to his convictions. The result was an absence of harmony well compensated by a conspicuous presence of variety—variety of a picturesque and entertaining sort.

All the riders were young gentlemen in fashionable society. If the reader has been wondering why it is that the ladies of New Orleans attend so humble an orgy as a mule-race, the thing is explained now. It is a fashion freak; all connected with it are people of fashion.

It is great fun, and cordially liked. The mule-race is one of the marked occasions of the year. It has brought some pretty fast mules to the front. One of these had to be ruled out, because he was so fast that he turned the thing into a one-mule contest, and robbed it of one of its best features—variety. But every now and then somebody disguises him with a new name and a new complexion, and rings him in again.

The riders dress in full jockey costumes of bright-colored silks, satins, and velvets.

The thirteen mules got away in a body, after a couple of false starts, and scampered off with prodigious spirit. As each mule and each rider had a distinct opinion of his own as to how the race ought to be run, and which side of the track was best in certain circumstances, and how often the track ought to be crossed, and when a collision ought to be accomplished, and when it ought to be avoided, these twenty-six conflicting opinions created a most fantastic and picturesque confusion, and the resulting spec-

115

tacle was killingly comical.

Mile heat; time, 2:22. Eight of the thirteen mules distanced. I had a bet on a mule which would have won if the procession had been reversed. The second heat was good fun; and so was the "consolation race for beaten mules," which followed later; but the first heat was the best in that respect.

I think that much the most enjoyable of all races is a steamboat race; but, next to that, I prefer the gay and joyous mule-rush.

THE RAVENS

One never tires of poking about in the dense woods that clothe all these lofty Neckar hills to their tops. The great deeps of a boundless forest have a beguiling and impressive charm in any country; but German legends and fairy tales have given these an added charm. They have peopled all that region with gnomes, and dwarfs, and all sorts of mysterious and uncanny creatures. At the time I am writing of, I had been reading so much of this literature that sometimes I was not sure but I was beginning to believe in the gnomes and fairies as realities.

One afternoon I got lost in the woods about a mile from the hotel, and presently fell into a train of dreamy thought about animals which talk, and kobolds, and enchanted folk, and the rest of the pleasant legendary stuff; and so, by stimulating my fancy, I finally got to imagining I glimpsed small flitting shapes here and there down the columned aisles of the forest. It was a place which was peculiarly meet for the occasion. It was a pine wood, with so thick and soft a carpet of brown needles that one's footfall made no more sound than if he were treading on wool; the tree-trunks were as round and straight and smooth as pillars, and stood close together; they were bare of branches to a point about twenty-five feet above-ground, and from there upward so thick with boughs that not a ray of sunlight could pierce through. The world was bright with sunshine outside, but a deep and mellow twilight reigned in there, and also a silence so profound that I seemed to hear my own breathings.

When I had stood ten minutes, thinking and imagining, and getting my spirit in tune with the place, and in the right mood to enjoy the supernatural, a raven suddenly uttered a horse croak over my head. It made me start; and then I was angry because I started. I looked up, and the creature was sitting on a limb right over me, looking down at me. I felt something of the same sense of humiliation and injury which one feels when he finds that a human stranger has been clandestinely inspecting him in his privacy and mentally commenting upon him. I eyed the raven, and the raven eyed me. Nothing was said during some seconds. Then the bird stepped a little way along his limb to get a better point of observation, lifted his wings, stuck his head far down below his shoulders toward me, and croaked again—a croak with a distinctly insulting expression about it. If he had spoken in English he could not have said any more plainly than he did say in raven, "Well, what do *you* want here?" I felt as foolish as if I had been caught in some mean act by a responsible being, and reproved for it. However, I made no reply; I would not bandy words with a raven. The adversary waited a while, with his shoulders still lifted, his head thrust down between them, and his keen bright eye fixed on me; then he threw out two or three more insults, which I could not understand, further than that I knew a portion of them consisted of language not used in church.

I still made no reply. Now the adversary raised his head and called. There was an answering croak from a little distance in the wood—evidently a croak of inquiry. The adversary explained with enthusiasm, and the other raven dropped everything and came. The two sat side by side on the limb and discussed me as freely and offensively as two great naturalists might discuss a new kind of bug. The thing became more and more embarrassing. They called in another friend. This was too much. I saw

that they had the advantage of me, and so I concluded to get out of the scrape by walking out of it. They enjoyed my defeat as much as any low white people could have done. They craned their necks and laughed at me (for a raven *can* laugh, just like a man), they squalled insulting remarks after me as long as they could see me. They were nothing but ravens—I knew that—what they thought about me could be a matter of no consequence—and yet when even a raven shouts after you, "What a hat!" "Oh, pull down your vest!" and that sort of thing, it hurts you and humiliates you, and there is no getting around it with fine reasoning and pretty arguments.

THE RETIRED MILK HORSE

We rode horseback all around the island of Hawaii (the crooked road making the distance two hundred miles), and enjoyed the journey very much. We were more than a week making the trip, because our Kanaka horses would not go by a house or a hut without stopping—whip and spur could not alter their minds about it, and so we finally found that it economized time to let them have their way. Upon inquiry the mystery was explained; the natives are such thoroughgoing gossips that they never pass a house without stopping to swap news, and consequently their horses learn to regard that sort of thing as an essential part of the whole duty of man, and his salvation not to be compassed without it. However, at a former crisis of my life I had once taken an aristocratic young lady out driving, behind a horse that had just retired from a long and honorable career as the moving impulse of a milk-wagon, and so this present experience awoke a reminiscent sadness in me in place of the exasperation more natural to the occasion. I remembered how helpless I was that day, and how humiliated; how ashamed I was of having intimated to the girl that I had always owned the horse and was accustomed to

grandeur; how hard I tried to appear easy, and even vivacious, under suffering that was consuming my vitals; how placidly and maliciously the girl smiled, and kept on smiling, while my hot blushes baked themselves into a permanent blood-pudding in my face; how the horse ambled from one side of the street to the other and waited

complacently before every third house two minutes and a quarter while I belabored his back and reviled him in my heart; how I tried to keep him from turning corners, and failed; how I moved heaven and earth to get him out of town, and did not succeed; how he traversed the entire settlement and delivered imaginary milk at a hundred and sixty-two different domiciles, and how he finally brought up at a dairy depot and refused to budge further, thus rounding and completing the revealment of what the plebeian service of his life had been; how, in eloquent silence, I walked the girl home, and how, when I took leave of her, her parting remark scorched my soul and appeared to blister me all over; she said that my horse was a fine, capable animal, and I must have taken great comfort in him in my time—but that if I would take along some milk-tickets next time, and appear to deliver them at the various halting-places, it might expedite his movements a little. There was a coolness between us after that.

RIDING THE AYAH

Aug. 16, 1895

Dear Kipling: It is reported that you are about to revisit India. This has moved me to journey to that far country in order that I may unload from my conscience a

debt long due you. Years ago you came from India to Elmira to visit me, as you said at the time. It has always been my purpose to return that visit and that great compliment, some day. I shall arrive next January, and you must be ready. I shall come riding my Ayah, with his tusks adorned with silver bells and ribbons, and escorted by a troop of native Howdahs, richly clad and mounted upon a herd of wild bungalows, and you must be on hand with a few bottles of ghee, for I shall be thirsty.

S

SEA-GOING CATS

Three big cats—very friendly loafers; they wander all over the ship; the white one follows the chief steward around like a dog. There is also a basket of kittens. One of these cats goes ashore, in port, in England, Australia, and India, to see how his various families are getting along, and is seen no more till the ship is ready to sail. No one knows how he finds out the sailing-date, but no doubt he comes down to the dock every day and takes a look, and when he sees baggage and passengers flocking in, recognizes that it is time to get aboard. This is what the sailors believe.

SEA-GOING RATS

Ours is a nice ship, roomy, comfortable, well ordered, and satisfactory. Now and then we step on a rat in a hotel, but we have had no rats on shipboard lately; unless, perhaps, in the *Flora*; we had more serious things to think of there, and did not notice. I have noticed that it is only in ships and hotels which still employ the odious Chinese gong, that you find rats. The reason would seem to be, that as a rat cannot tell the time of day by a clock, he won't stay where he cannot find out when dinner is ready.

SHARKS OR MEN?

It is a fine race, the Fijians, with brains in their heads and an inquiring turn of mind. It appears that their savage ancestors had a doctrine of immortality in their scheme of religion—with limitations. That is to say, their dead friend would go to a happy hereafter if he could be accumulated, but not otherwise. They drew the line; they thought that the missionary's doctrine was too sweeping, too comprehensive. They called his attention to certain facts. For instance, many of their friends had been devoured by sharks; the sharks, in their turn, were caught and eaten by other men; later, these men were captured in war, and eaten by the enemy. The original persons had entered into the composition of the sharks; next, they and the sharks had become part of the flesh and blood and bone of the cannibals. How, then, could the particles of the original men be searched out from the final conglomerate and put together again? The inquirers were full of doubts, and considered that the missionary had not examined the matter with the gravity and attention which so serious a thing deserved.

SNAKES AND BATS

Along outside of the front fence ran the country road, dusty in the summertime, and a good place for snakes—they liked to lie in it and sun themselves; when they were rattlesnakes or puff adders, we killed them; when they were black snakes, or racers, or belonged to the fabled "hoop" breed, we fled, without shame; when they were "house snakes" or "garters," we carried them home and put them in Aunt Patsy's work basket for a surprise; for she was prejudiced against snakes, and always when she

took the basket in her lap and they began to climb out of it it disordered her mind. She never could seem to get used to them; her opportunities went for nothing. And she was always cold toward bats, too, and could not bear them; and yet I think a bat is as friendly a bird as there is. My mother was Aunt Patsy's sister and had the same wild superstitions. A bat is beautifully soft and silky; I do not know any creature that is pleasanter to the touch or is more grateful for caressings, if offered in the right spirit. I know all about these coleoptera, because our great cave, three miles below Hannibal, was multitudinously stocked with them, and often I brought them home to amuse my mother with. It was easy to manage if it was a school day, because then I had ostensibly been to school and hadn't any bats. She was not a suspicious person, but full of trust and confidence; and when I said, "There's something in my coat pocket for you," she would put her hand in. But she always took it out again, herself; I didn't have to tell her. It was remarkable, the way she couldn't learn to like private bats. The more experience she had, the more she could not change her views.

THE SWISS CHAMOIS

Next morning we left in the train for Switzerland, and reached Lucerne about ten o'clock at night. The first discovery I made was that the beauty of the lake had not been exaggerated. Within a day or two I made another discovery. This was, that the lauded chamois is not a wild goat; that it is not a horned animal; that it is not shy; that it does not avoid human society; and that there is no peril in hunting it. The chamois is a black or brown creature no bigger than a mustard seed; you do not have to go after it, it comes after you; it arrives in vast herds and skips and scampers all over your body, inside your clothes; thus it is not shy, but extremely sociable; it is not afraid of man, on the contrary, it will attack him; its bite is not dangerous, but neither is it pleasant; its activity has not been overstated—if you try to put your finger on it, it will skip a thousand times its own length at one jump, and no eye is sharp enough to see where it lights. A great deal of romantic nonsense has been written about the Swiss chamois and the perils of hunting it, whereas the truth is that even women and children hunt it, and fearlessly; indeed, everybody hunts it; the hunting is going on all the time, day and night, in bed and out of it. It is poetic foolishness to hunt it with a gun; very few people

do that; there is not one man in a million who can hit it with a gun. It is much easier to catch it than it is to shoot it, and only the experienced chamois-hunter can do either. Another common piece of exaggeration is that about the "scarcity" of the chamois. It is the reverse of scarce. Droves of one hundred million chamois are not unusual in the Swiss hotels. Indeed, they are so numerous as to be a great pest. The romancers always dress up the chamois-hunter in a fanciful and picturesque costume, whereas the best way to hunt this game is to do it without any costume at all. The article of commerce called chamois-skin is another fraud; nobody could skin a chamois, it is too small. The creature is a humbug in every way, and everything which has been written about it is sentimental exaggeration. It was no pleasure to me to find the chamois out, for he had been one of my pet illusions; all my life it had been my dream to see him in his native wilds some day, and engage in the adventurous sport of chasing him from cliff to cliff. It is no pleasure to me to expose him, now, and destroy the reader's delight in him and respect for him, but still it must be done, for when an honest writer discovers an imposition it is his simple duty to strip it bare and hurl it down from its place of honor, no matter who suffers by it; any other course would render him unworthy of the public confidence.

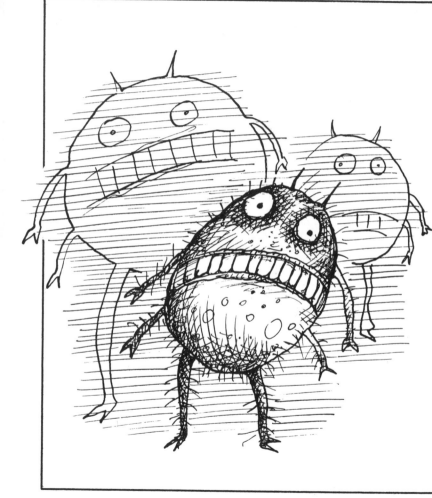

TARANTULAS!

The surveyors brought back more tarantulas with them, and so we had quite a menagerie arranged along the shelves of the room. Some of these spiders could straddle over a common saucer with their hairy, muscular legs, and when their feelings were hurt, or their dignity offended, they were the wickedest-looking desperadoes the animal world can furnish. If their glass prison-houses were touched ever so lightly they were up and spoiling for a fight in a minute. Starchy?—proud? Indeed, they would take up a straw and pick their teeth like a member of Congress. There was as usual a furious "zephyr" blowing the first night of the Brigade's return, and about midnight the roof of an adjoining stable blew off, and a corner of it came crashing through the side of our ranch. There was a simultaneous awakening, and a tumultuous muster of the Brigade in the dark, and a general tumbling and sprawling over each other in the narrow aisle between the bed-rows. In the midst of the turmoil, Bob H—— sprung up out of a sound sleep, and knocked down a shelf with his head. Instantly he shouted:

"Turn out, boys—the tarantulas is loose!"

No warning ever sounded so dreadful. Nobody tried, any longer, to leave the room, lest he might step on a tarantula. Every man groped for a trunk or a bed, and jumped on it. Then followed the strangest silence—a silence of grisly suspense it was, too—waiting, expectancy, fear. It was as dark as pitch, and one had to imagine the spectacle of those fourteen scant-clad men roosting gingerly on trunks and beds, for not a thing could be seen. Then came occasional little interruptions of the silence, and one could recognize a man and tell his locality by his voice, or locate any other sound a sufferer made by his gropings or changes of position. The occasional voices were not given to much speaking—you simply heard a gentle ejaculation of "Ow!" followed by a solid thump, and you knew the gentleman had felt a hairy blanket or something touch his bare skin and had skipped from a bed to the floor. Another silence. Presently you would hear a gasping voice say:

"Su-su-something's crawling up the back of my neck!"

Every now and then you could hear a little subdued scramble and a sorrowful "O Lord!" and then you knew that somebody was getting away from something he took for a tarantula, and not losing any time about it, either. Directly a voice in the corner rang out wild and clear:

"I've got him! I've got him!" [Pause, and probable change of circumstances.] "No, he's got me! Oh, ain't they *never* going to fetch a lantern!"

The lantern came at that moment, in the hands of

Mrs. O'Flannigan, whose anxiety to know the amount of damage done by the assaulting roof had not prevented her waiting a judicious interval, after getting out of bed and lighting up, to see if the wind was done, now, up-stairs, or had a larger contract.

The landscape presented when the lantern flashed into the room was picturesque, and might have been funny to some people, but was not to us. Although we were perched so strangely upon boxes, trunks and beds, and so strangely attired, too, we were too earnestly distressed and too genuinely miserable to see any fun about it, and there was not the semblance of a smile anywhere visible. I know I am not capable of suffering more than I did during those few minutes of suspense in the dark, surrounded by those creeping, bloody-minded tarantulas. I had skipped from bed to bed and from box to box in a cold agony, and every time I touched anything that was fuzzy I fancied I felt the fangs. I had rather go to war than live that episode over again. Nobody was hurt. The man who thought a tarantula had "got him" was mistaken—only a crack in a box had caught his finger. Not one of those escaped tarantulas was ever seen again. There were ten or twelve of them. We took candles and hunted the place high and low for them, but with no success. Did we go back to bed then? We did nothing of the kind. Money could not have persuaded us to do it. We sat up the rest of the night playing cribbage and keeping a sharp lookout for the enemy.

TOM QUARTZ

One of my comrades—another of those victims of eighteen years of unrequited toil and blighted hopes—was one of the gentlest spirits that ever bore its patient cross in a weary exile: grave and simple Dick Baker, pocket-miner of Dead-Horse Gulch. He was forty-six, gray as a rat, earnest, thoughtful, slenderly educated, slouchily dressed, and clay-soiled, but his heart was finer metal than any gold his shovel ever brought to light—than any, indeed, that ever was mined or minted.

Whenever he was out of luck and a little downhearted, he would fall to mourning over the loss of a wonderful cat he used to own (for where women and children are not, men of kindly impulses take up with pets, for they must love something). And he always spoke of the strange sagacity of that cat with the air of a man who believed in his secret heart that there was something human about it—maybe even supernatural.

I heard him talking about this animal once. He said:

"Gentlemen, I used to have a cat here, by the name of Tom Quartz, which you'd 'a' took an interest in, I reckon—most anybody would. I had him here eight year—and he was the remarkablest cat *I* ever see. He was a large gray one of the Tom specie, an' he had more hard, natchral sense than any man in this camp—'n' a *power* of dignity—he wouldn't let the Gov'ner of Californy be familiar with him. He never ketched a rat in his life—'peared to be above it. He never cared for nothing but mining. He knowed more about mining, that cat did, than any man *I* ever, ever see. You couldn't tell *him* noth'n' 'bout placer-diggin's—'n' as for pocket-mining, why he was just born for it. He would dig out after me an' Jim when we went over the hills prospect'n', and he would trot along behind us for as much as five mile, if we went so fur. An' he had the best judgment about mining-ground—why you never see anything like it. When we went to work, he'd scatter a glance around, 'n' if he didn't think much of the indications, he would give a look as much as to say, 'Well, I'll have to get you to excuse *me*,' 'n' without another word he'd hyste his nose into the air 'n' shove for home. But if the ground suited him, he would lay low 'n' keep dark till the first pan was washed, 'n' then he would sidle up 'n' take a look, an' if there was about six or seven grains of gold *he* was satisfied—he didn't want no better prospect 'n' that—'n'

then he would lay down on our coats and snore like a steamboat till we'd struck the pocket, an' then get up 'n' superintend. He was nearly lightnin' on superintending.

"Well, by an' by, up comes this yer quartz excitement. Everybody was into it—everybody was pick'n 'n' blast'n' instead of shovelin' dirt on the hillside—everybody was put'n' down a shaft instead of scrapin' the surface. Noth'n' would do Jim, but *we* must tackle the ledges, too, 'n' so we did. We commenced putt'n' down a shaft, 'n' Tom Quartz he begin to wonder what in the dickens it was all about. *He* hadn't ever seen any mining like that before, 'n' he was all upset, as you may say—he couldn't come to a right understanding of it no way—it was too many for *him*. He was down on it, too, you bet you—he was down on it powerful—'n' always appeared to consider it the cussedest foolishness out. But that cat, you know, was *always* agin new-fangled arrangements—somehow he never could abide 'em. *You* know how it is with old habits. But by an' by Tom Quartz begin to git sort of reconciled a little, though he never *could* altogether understand that eternal sinkin' of a shaft an' never pannin' out anything. At last he got to comin' down in the shaft, hisself, to try to cipher it out. An' when he'd git the blues, 'n' feel kind o' scruffy, 'n' aggravated 'n' disgusted—knowin' as he did, that the bills was runnin' up all the time an' we warn't makin' a cent—he would curl up on a gunny-sack in the corner an' go to sleep. Well, one day when the shaft was down about eight foot, the rock got so hard that we had to put in a blast—the first blast'n' we'd ever done since Tom Quartz was born. An' then we lit the fuse 'n' clumb out 'n' got off 'bout fifty yards—'n' forgot 'n' left Tom Quartz sound asleep on the gunny-sack. In 'bout a minute we seen a puff of smoke bust up out of the hole, 'n' then everything let go with an awful crash, 'n' about four million ton of rocks 'n' dirt 'n' smoke 'n' splinters shot up 'bout a mile an' a half into the air, an' by George, right in the dead center of it was old Tom Quartz a-goin' end over end, an' a-snortin' an' a-sneez'n', an' a-clawin' an' a-reachin' for things like all possessed. But it warn't no use, you know, it warn't no use. An' that was the last we see of *him* for about two minutes 'n' a half, an' then all of a sudden it begin to rain rocks and rubbage, an' directly he come down ker-whop about ten foot off f'm where we stood. Well, I reckon he was p'raps the orneriest-lookin' beast you ever see. One ear was sot back on his neck, 'n' his tail was stove up, 'n' his eye-winkers was swinged off, 'n' he was all blacked up with powder an' smoke, an' all sloppy with mud 'n' slush f'm one end to the other. Well, sir, it warn't no use to try to apologize—we couldn't say a word. He took a sort of a disgusted look at hisself, 'n' then he looked at us—an' it was just exactly the same as if he had said—

'Gents, maybe *you* think it's smart to take advantage of a cat that ain't had no experience of quartz-minin', but *I* think *different*'—an' then he turned on his heel 'n' marched off home without ever saying another word.

"That was jest his style. An' maybe you won't believe it, but after that you never see a cat so prejudiced agin quartz-mining as what he was. An' by an' by when he *did* get to goin' down in the shaft ag'in, you'd 'a' been astonished at his sagacity. The minute we'd tetch off a blast 'n' the fuse'd begin to sizzle, he'd give a look as much as to say, 'Well, I'll have to git you to excuse *me*,' an' it was surpris'n' the way he'd shin out of that hole 'n' go f'r a tree. Sagacity? It ain't no name for it. 'Twas *inspiration!*"

I said, "Well, Mr. Baker, his prejudice against quartz-mining *was* remarkable, considering how he came by it. Couldn't you ever cure him of it?"

"*Cure him!* No! When Tom Quartz was sot once, he was *always* sot—and you might 'a' blowed him up as much as three million times 'n' you'd never 'a' broken him of his cussed prejudice agin quartz-mining."

The affection and the pride that lit up Baker's face when he delivered this tribute to the firmness of his humble friend of other days, will always be a vivid memory with me.

134

U

UNCLE LEM'S COMPOSITE DOG

"You look at my Uncle Lem—what do you say to that? That's all I ask you—you just look at my Uncle Lem and talk to me about accidents! It was like this: one day my Uncle Lem and his dog was downtown, and he was a-leanin' up against a scaffolding—sick, or drunk, or somethin'—and there was an Irishman with a hod of bricks up the ladder along about the third story, and his foot slipped and down he come, bricks and all, and hit a stranger fair and square and knocked the everlasting aspirations out of him; he was ready for the coroner in two minutes. Now them people said it was an accident.

"Accident! there warn't no accident about it; 'twas a special providence, and had a mysterious, noble intention back of it. The idea was to save that Irishman. If the stranger hadn't been there that Irishman would have been killed. The people said 'special providence—sho! the dog was there—why didn't the Irishman fall on the dog? Why warn't the dog app'inted?' Fer a mighty good reason—the dog would 'a' seen him a-coming; you can't depend on no dog to carry out a special providence. You couldn't hit a dog with an Irishman because—lemme see, what was that dog's name . . . (musing) . . . oh, yes, Jasper—and a mighty good dog too; he wa'n't no common dog, he wa'n't no mongrel; he was a composite. A composite dog is a dog that's made up of all the valuable qualities that's in the dog breed—kind of a syndicate; and a mongrel is made up of the riffraff that's left over. That Jasper was one of the most wonderful dogs you ever see. Uncle Lem got him off the Wheelers. I reckon you've heard of the Wheelers; ain't no better blood south of the line than the Wheelers.

UN-NATURAL HISTORY

I think it is not wise for an emperor, or a king, or a president, to come down into the boxing ring, so to speak, and lower the dignity of his office by meddling in the small affairs of private citizens. I think it is not even discreet in a private citizen to come out in public and make a large noise, and by criticism and faultfinding try to cough down and injure another citizen whose trade he knows nothing valuable about. It seems to me that natural history is a pretty poor thing to squabble about anyway, because it is not an exact science. What we know about it is built out of the careful or careless observations of students of animal nature, and no man can be accurate enough in his observations to safely pose as the last and unassailable authority in the matter—not even Aristotle, not even Pliny, not even Sir John Mandeville, not even Jonah, not even Theodore Roosevelt.

All these professionals ought to stand ready to accept each other's facts, closing one eye furtively now and then, perhaps, but keeping strictly quiet and saying nothing. The professional who disputes another professional's facts damages the business and imperils his own statistics,

there being no statistics connected with the business that are absolute and unassailable. The only wise and safe course is for all the naturalists to stand by each other and accept and endorse every discovery, or seeming discovery, that any one of them makes. Mr. Roosevelt is immeasurably indiscreet. He accepts as an established fact that the ravens fed Elijah; it is then bad policy in him to question the surgical ability of Mr. Long's bird.* I accept the raven's work, and admire it. I know the raven; I know him well; I know he has no disposition to share his food, inferior and overdue as it is, with prophets or presidents or any one else—yet I feel that it would not be right nor judicious in me to question the validity of the hospitalities of those ravens while trying to market natural-history marvels of my own which are of a similar magnitude.

I know of a turkey hen that tried during several weeks to hatch out a porcelain egg, then the gobbler took the job and sat on that egg two entire summers and at last hatched it. He hatched out of it a doll's tea set of fourteen pieces, and all perfect except that the teapot had no spout, on account of the material running out. I know this to be true, of my own personal knowledge, and I do as Mr. Roosevelt and Mr. Burroughs and Jonah and Aristotle, and all the other naturalists do—that is to say, I merely make assertions and back them up with just my say-so,

offering no other evidence of any kind. I personally know that that unusual thing happened; I knew the turkey; I furnished the egg and I have got the crockery. It establishes, once and for all, the validity of Mr. Long's statement about his bird—because it is twice as remarkable as that bird's performance and yet it happened. If I must speak plainly, I think it is rank folly for the President, or John Burroughs, or any other professional, to try to bear any other naturalist's stock in the public market. It is all watered—I even regard some of my own discoveries in that light—and so it is but common prudence for those of us who got in on the ground floor to refrain from boring holes in it.

*The Rev. Doctor Long was a popular naturalist of the period who had witnessed a wild bird mending its broken leg with a self-made cast.—ED.

138

V

THE VOICE
OF THE TURTLE

He was just in the act of throwing a clod at a mud-turtle which was sunning itself on a small log in the brook. We said:

"Don't do that, Jack. What do you want to harm him for? What has he done?"

"Well, then, I won't kill him, but I ought to, because he is a fraud."

We asked him why, but he said it was no matter. We asked him why, once or twice, as we walked back to the camp, but he still said it was no matter. But late at night, when he was sitting in a thoughtful mood on the bed, we asked him again and he said:

"Well, it don't matter; I don't mind it now, but I did not like it to-day, you know, because *I* don't tell anything that isn't so, and I don't think the Colonel ought to, either. But he did; he told us at prayers in the Pilgrims' tent, last night, and he seemed as if he was reading it out of the Bible, too, about this country flowing with milk and honey, and about the voice of the turtle being heard in the land. I thought that was drawing it a little strong, about the turtles, anyhow, but I asked Mr. Church if it was so, and he said it was, and what Mr. Church tells me, I believe. But I sat there and watched that turtle nearly an hour to-day, and I almost burned up in the sun; but I never heard him sing. I believe I sweated a double handful of sweat—I *know* I did—because it got in my eyes, and it was running down over my nose all the time; and you know my pants are tighter than anybody else's—Paris foolishness—and the buckskin seat of them got wet with sweat, and then got dry again and began to draw up and pinch and tear loose—it was awful—but I never heard him sing. Finally I said, This is a fraud— that is what it is, it is a fraud—and if I had had any sense I might have known a cursed mud-turtle couldn't sing. And then I said, I don't wish to be hard on this fellow, and I will just give him ten minutes to commence; ten minutes—and then if he don't, down goes his building. But he *didn't* commence, you know. I had stayed there all that time, thinking maybe he might, pretty soon, because he kept on raising his head up and letting it down, and drawing the skin over his eyes for a minute and then opening them out again, as if he was trying to study up something to sing, but just as the ten minutes were up and I was all beat out and blistered, he laid his blamed head down on a knot and went fast asleep."

"It *was* a little hard, after you had waited so long."

"I should think so. I said, Well, if you won't sing, you sha'n't sleep, anyway; and if you fellows had let me alone

I would have made him shin out of Galilee quicker than any turtle ever did yet. But it isn't any matter now—let it go. The skin is all off the back of my neck."

THE VULTURE

A vulture on board; bald, red, queer-shaped head, featherless red places here and there on his body, intense great black eyes set in featherless rims of inflamed flesh; dissipated look; a businesslike style, a selfish, conscienceless, murderous aspect—the very look of a professional assassin, and yet a bird which does no murder. What was the use of getting him up in that tragic style for so innocent a trade as his? For this one isn't the sort that wars upon the living, his diet is offal—and the more out of date it is the better he likes it. Nature should give him a suit of rusty black; then he would be all right, for he would look like an undertaker and would harmonize with his business; whereas the way he is now he is horribly out of true.

WAR HORSES

We occupied an old maple-sugar camp, whose half-rotted troughs were still propped against the trees. A long corn-crib served for sleeping-quarters for the battalion. On our left, half a mile away, were Mason's farm and house; and he was a friend to the cause. Shortly after noon the farmers began to arrive from several directions, with mules and horses for our use, and these they lent us for as long as the war might last, which they judged would be about three months. The animals were of all sizes, all colors, and all breeds. They were mainly young and frisky, and nobody in the command could stay on them long at a time; for we were town boys, and ignorant of horsemanship. The creature that fell to my share was a very small mule, and yet so quick and active that it could throw me without difficulty; and it did this whenever I got on it. Then it would bray—stretching its neck out, laying its ears back, and spreading its jaws till you could see down to its works. It was a disagreeable animal in every way. If I took it by the bridle and tried to lead it off the grounds, it would sit down and brace back, and no one could budge it. However, I was not entirely destitute of military resources, and I did presently manage to spoil this game; for I had seen many a steamboat aground in my time, and knew a trick or two which even a grounded mule would be obliged to respect. There was a well by the corn-crib; so I substituted thirty fathom of rope for the bridle, and fetched him home with the windlass.

I will anticipate here sufficiently to say that we did learn to ride, after some days' practice, but never well. We could not learn to like our animals; they were not choice ones, and most of them had annoying peculiarities of one kind or another. Stevens's horse would carry him, when he was not noticing, under the huge excrescences which form on the trunks of oak-trees, and wipe him out of the saddle; in this way Stevens got several bad hurts. Sergeant Bowers's horse was very large and tall, with slim, long legs, and looked like a railroad bridge. His size enabled him to reach all about, and as far as he wanted to, with his head; so he was always biting Bowers's legs. On the march, in the sun, Bowers slept a good deal; and as soon as the horse recognized that he was asleep he would reach around and bite him on the leg. His legs were black and blue with bites. This was the only thing that could ever make him swear, but this always did; whenever his horse bit him he always swore, and of course Stevens, who laughed at everything, laughed at this, and would even get into such convulsions over it as to lose his balance and fall off his horse; and then Bowers, already irritated by the pain of the horse-bite, would resent the laughter with hard language, and there would be a quarrel; so that horse made no end of trouble and bad blood in the command.

WHEN RATS LEAVE THE SHIP

"Speaking of rats, once in Honolulu me and old Josephus—got rich as Croesus in San F. afterwards—we were going home as passengers from the S.I.* in a brand-new brig on her 3rd voyage—and our trunks were down below. He went with me—laid over one vessel to do it—because he warn't no sailor and he liked to be with a man that was—and the brig was sliding out between the buoys and her head-line was paying out ashore. There was a wood-pile right where the line was made fast to the pier, and up come the damndest biggest rat—as big as an

*Sandwich Islands (or Hawaii).—ED.

ordinary cat he was—and darted out on that line and cantered for the shore—and up came another—and another—and another—and away they galloped over that hawser—each one treading on t'other's tail till they were so thick that you couldn't see a thread of the cable, and there was a procession of 'em 200 yards long over the levee like a streak of ants—and the Kanakas, some throwing sticks from that wood-pile and chunks of lava and coral at 'em and knocking 'em endways and every which way. But do you s'pose it made any difference to them rats? Not a particle—not a particle, bless your soul—they never let up till the last rat was ashore out of that brand-new beautiful brig. I called a Kanaka with his boat, and he hove alongside and shinned up a rope and says I: 'Do you see that trunk down there?' 'Ai.' 'Clatter it ashore as

quick as God'll let you.'

"Josephus says: 'What are you doing, Captain?' and I says: 'Doing? Why I'm a-taking my trunk ashore, that's what I'm a-doing!'

" 'Taking your trunk ashore? Why bless us what is that for?'

" 'What is it for?' says I—'Do you see them rats? Do you notice them rats a-leaving this ship? She's doomed, Sir—she's doomed! Burnt brandy wouldn't save her, Sir! She'll never finish this voyage. She'll never be heard of again, Sir.'

"Josephus says: 'Boy, take that other trunk ashore too.'

"And don't you know, Sir, that brig sailed out of Honolulu without a rat aboard and was never seen again by mortal man, Sir."

XYZ

A CAT TALE*

*Mark Twain's animals seem to have stopped at W. There are no X, Y, and Z animals of consequence that the present editor can locate; and he believes that Twain was just *lazy* and careless, as he was so often, in not finishing up his Bestiary decently. As a matter of fact Sam Clemens was notorious for not having good endings in his prose fictions, and some of his endings were positively bad, as in *Huck Finn*, and *The Mysterious Stranger*.

In this case we have been able to correct his carelessness by inserting, as a most appropriate ending indeed, "A Cat's Tail," in these pages.—ED.

My little girls—Susy, aged eight, and Clara, six—often require me to help them go to sleep, nights, by telling them original tales. They think my tales are better than paregoric, and quicker. While I talk, they make comments and ask questions, and we have a pretty good time. I thought maybe other little people might like to try one of my narcotics—so I offer this one.

—M.T.

Once there was a noble big cat, whose Christian name was Catasauqua—because she lived in that region—but she did not have any surname, because she was a short-tailed cat—being a Manx—and did not need one. It is very just and becoming in a long-tailed cat to have a surname, but it would be very ostentatious, and even dishonorable, in a Manx. Well, Catasauqua had a beautiful family of catlings; and they were of different colors, to harmonize with their characters. Cattaraugus, the eldest, was white, and he had high impulses and a pure heart; Catiline, the youngest, was black, and he had a self-seeking nature, his motives were nearly always base, he was truculent and insincere. He was vain and foolish, and often said he would rather be what he was, and live like a bandit, yet have none above him, than be a cat-'o-nine-tails and eat with the King. He hated his harmless and unoffending little catercousins, and frequently drove them from his presence with imprecations, and at times even resorted to violence.

SUSY: What are catercousins, Papa?

Quarter-cousins—it is so set down in the big dictionary. You observe I refer to it every now and then. This is because I do not wish to make any mistakes, my purpose being to instruct as well as entertain. Whenever I use a word which you do not understand, speak up and I will look and find out what it means. But do not interrupt me except for cause, for I am always excited when I am erecting history, and want to get on. Well, one day Catasauqua met with a misfortune; her house burned down. It

151

was the very day after it had been insured for double its value, too—how singular! Yes, and how lucky! This often happens. It teaches us that mere loading a house down with insurance isn't going to save it. Very well, Catasauqua took the insurance money and built a new house; and a much better one, too; and what is more, she had money left to add a gaudy concatenation of extra improvements with. Oh, I tell you! What she didn't know about catallactics no other cat need ever try to acquire.

CLARA: What is catallactics, Papa?

The dictionary intimates, in a nebulous way, that it is a sort of demi-synonym for the science commonly called political economy.

CLARA: Thank you, Papa.

Yes, behind the house she constructed a splendid large catadrome, and enclosed it with a caterwaul about nine feet high, and in the center was a spacious grass plot where—

CLARA: What is a catadrome, Papa?

I will look. Ah, it is a race course; I thought it was a ten-pin alley. But no matter; in fact, it is all the better; for cats do not play ten-pins, when they are feeling well, but they *do* run races, you know; and the spacious grass plot was for cat fights, and other free exhibitions; and for ball games—three-cornered cat, and all that sort of thing;

a lovely spot, lovely. Yes, indeed; it had a hedge of dainty little catkins around it, and right in the center was a splendid great categorematic in full leaf, and—

SUSY: What is a categorematic, Papa?

I think it's a kind of a shade tree, but I'll look. No—I was mistaken; it is a *word*: "a word which is capable of being employed by itself as a term."

SUSY: Thank you, Papa.

Don't mention it. Yes, you see, it wasn't a shade tree; the good Catasauqua didn't know that, else she wouldn't have planted it right there in the way; you can't run over a word like that, you know, and not cripple yourself more or less. Now don't forget that definition, it may come handy to you some day—there is no telling—life is full of vicissitudes. Always remember, a categorematic is a word which a cat can use by herself as a term; but she mustn't try to use it along with another cat, for that is not the idea. Far from it. We have authority for it, you see—Mr. Webster; and he is dead, too, besides. It would be a noble good thing if his dictionary was, too. But that is too much to expect. Yes; well, Catasauqua filled her house with internal improvements—catcalls in every room, and they are Oh, ever so much handier than bells; and catamounts to mount the stairs with, instead of those troublesome elevators which are always getting out of order; and civet cats in the kitchen, in place of the ordinary sieves, which you can't ever sift anything with, in a satisfactory way; and a couple of tidy ash cats to clean out the stove and keep it in order; and—catenated on the roof—an alert and cultivated polecat to watch the flagpole and keep the banner a-flying. Ah, yes—such was Catasauqua's country residence; and she named it Kamscatka—after her dear native land far away.

CLARA: What is catenated, Papa?

Chained, my child. The polecat was attached by a chain to some object upon the roof contiguous to the flagpole. This was to retain him in his position.

CLARA: Thank you, Papa.

The front garden was a spectacle of sublime and bewildering magnificence. A stately row of flowering catalpas stretched from the front door clear to the gate, wreathed from stem to stern with the delicate tendrils and shining scales of the cat's-foot ivy, whilst ever and anon the enchanted eye wondered from congeries of lordly cattails and kindred catapetalous blooms too deep for utterance, only to encounter the still more entrancing vision of catnip without number and without price, and swoon away in ecstasy unutterable, under the blissful intoxication of its too, too fragrant breath!

BOTH CHILDREN: Oh, how lovely!

You may well say it. Few there be that shall look upon the like again. Yet was not this all; for hither to the north boiled the majestic cataract in unimaginable grandiloquence, and thither to the south sparkled the gentle catadupe in serene and incandescent tranquility, whilst far and near the halcyon brooklet flowed between!

BOTH CHILDREN: Oh, how sweet! What is a catadupe, Papa?

Small waterfall, my darlings. Such is Webster's belief. All things being in readiness for the housewarming, the widow sent out her invitations, and then proceeded with her usual avocations. For Catasauqua was a widow—sorrow cometh to us all. The husband-cat—Catullus was his name—was no more. He was of a lofty character, brave to rashness, and almost incredibly unselfish. He gave eight of his lives for his country, reserving only one for himself. Yes, the banquet having been ordered, the good Catasauqua tuned up for the customary morning-song, accompanying herself on the catarrh, and her little ones joined in.

These were the words:

There was a little cat,
And she caught a little rat,
Which she dutifully rendered to her mother,
Who said "Bake him in a pie,
For his flavor's rather high—
Or confer him on the poor, if you'd druther."

Catasauqua sang soprano, Catiline sang tenor, Cattaraugus sang bass. It was exquisite melody; it would make your hair stand right up.

SUSY: Why, Papa, I didn't know cats could sing.

Oh, can't they, though! Well, these could. Cats are packed full of music—just as full as they can hold; and when they die, people remove it from them and sell it to the fiddle-makers. Oh, yes indeed. Such is Life.

SUSY: Oh, here is a picture! Is it a picture of the music, Papa?

Only the eye of prejudice could doubt it, my child.

SUSY: Did you draw it, Papa?

I am indeed the author of it.

SUSY: How wonderful! What is a picture like this called, Papa?

A work of art, my child. There—do not hold it so close; prop it up on the chair, *three steps away*; now then—that is right; you see how much better and stronger the expression is than when it is close by. It is because some of this picture is drawn in perspective.

CLARA: Did you always know how to draw, Papa?

Yes. I was born so. But of course I could not draw at first as well as I can now. These things require study—and practice. Mere talent is not sufficient. It takes a person a long time to get so he can draw a picture like this.

CLARA: How long did it take you, Papa?

Many years—thirty years, I reckon. Off and on—for I did not devote myself exclusively to art. Still, I have had a great deal of practice. Ah, practice is the great thing! It accomplishes wonders. Before I was twenty-five, I had got so I could draw a cork as well as anybody that ever was. And many a time I have drawn a blank in a lottery. Once I drew a check that wouldn't go; and after the war I tried to draw a pension, but this was too ambitious. However, the most gifted must fail sometimes. Do you observe those things that are sticking up, in this picture? They are not bones, they are paws; it is very hard to express the difference between bones and paws, in a picture.

SUSY: Which is Cattaraugus, Papa?

The little pale one that almost has the end of his mother's tail in his mouth.

SUSY: But, Papa, that tail is not right. You know Cata-

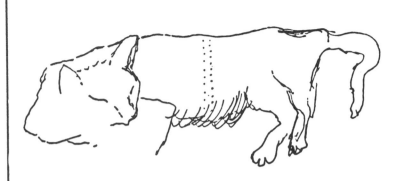

sauqua was a Manx, and had a short one.

It is a just remark, my child; but a long tail was necessary, here, to express a certain passion, the passion of joy. Therefore the insertion of a long tail is permissible; it is called a poetic license. You cannot express the passion of joy with a short tail. Nor even extraordinary excitement. You notice that Cattaraugus is brilliantly excited; now nearly all of that verve, spirit, *élan*, is owing to his tail; yet if I had been false to art to be true to Nature, you would see there nothing but a poor little stiff and emotionless stump on that cat that would have cast a coldness over the whole scene; yet Cattaraugus was a Manx, like his mother, and had hardly any more tail than a rabbit. Yes, in art, the office of the tail is to express feeling; so, if you wish to portray a cat in repose, you will

always succeed better by leaving out the tail. Now here is a striking illustration of the very truth which I am trying to impress upon you. I proposed to draw a cat recumbent and in repose; but just as I had finished the front end of her, she got up and began to gaze passionately at a bird and wriggle her tail in a most expressively wistful way. I had to finish her with that end standing, and the other end lying. It greatly injures the picture. For, you see, it confuses two passions together—the passion of standing up, and the passion of lying down. These are incompatible; and they convey a bad effect to the picture by rendering it unrestful to the eye. In my opinion a cat in a picture ought to be doing one thing or the other, lying down or standing up, but not both. I ought to have laid this one down again, and put a brick or something on her; but I did not think of it at the time. Let us now separate these conflicting passions in this cat, so that you can see each by itself, and the more easily study it. Lay your hand on the picture, to where I have made those dots, and cover the rear half of it from sight—now you observe how reposeful the front end is. Very well; now lay your hand on the front end and cover *it* from sight—do you observe the eager wriggle in that tail? It is a wriggle which only the presence of a bird can inspire.

SUSY: You must know a wonderful deal, Papa.

I have that reputation—in Europe; but here the best

155

minds think I am superficial. However, I am content; I make no defense; my pictures show what I am.

SUSY: Papa, I should think you would take pupils.

No, I have no desire for riches. Honest poverty and a conscience torpid through virtuous inaction are more to me than corner lots and praise.

But to resume. The morning-song being over, Catasauqua told Catiline and Cattaraugus to fetch their little books, and she would teach them how to spell.

BOTH CHILDREN: Why, Papa! Do cats have books?

Yes, catechisms. Just so. Facts are stubborn things. After lesson, Catasauqua gave Catiline and Cattaraugus some rushes, so that they could earn a little circus-money by building cat's cradles, and at the same time amuse themselves and not miss her; then she went to the kitchen and dining room to inspect the preparations for the banquet.

The moment her back was turned, Catiline put down his work and got out his catpipe for a smoke.

SUSY: Why, how naughty!

Thou hast well spoken. It was disobedience; and disobedience is the flagship of the fleet of sin. The gentle Cattaraugus sighed and said: "For shame, Catiline! How often has our dear mother told you not to do that! Ah, how can you thus disregard the commandments of the author of your being!"

SUSY: Why, what beautiful language, for such a little thing, *wasn't* it, Papa?

Ah, yes, indeed. That was the kind of cat he was—cultivated, you see. He had sat at the feet of Rollo's mother; and in the able "Franconia Series" he had not failed to observe how harmoniously gigantic language and a microscopic topic go together. Catiline heard his brother through, and then replied with the contemptuous ejaculation: "S'scat!"

It means the same that Shakespeare means when he says, "Go to." Nevertheless, Catiline's conscience was not at rest. He murmured something about Where was the harm, since his mother would never know? But Cattaraugus said, sweetly but sadly, "Alas, if we but do the right under restraint of authoritative observance, where then is the merit?"

SUSY: How *good* he was!

Monumentally so. The more we contemplate his character, the more sublime it appears. But Catiline, who was coarse and worldly, hated all lofty sentiments, and especially such as were stated in choice and lofty terms; he wished to resent this one, yet compelled himself to hold his peace; but when Cattaraugus said it over again, partly to enjoy the sound of it, but mainly for his brother's good, Catiline lost his patience, and said, "Oh, take a walk!"

Yet he still felt badly; for he knew he was doing wrong. He began to pretend he did not know it was against the rule to smoke his catpipe; but Cattaraugus, without an utterance, lifted an accusing paw toward the wall, where, among the illuminated mottoes, hung this one:

"NO SMOKING. STRICTLY PROHIBITED."

Catiline turned pale; and, murmuring in a broken voice, "I am undone—forgive me, Brother," laid the fatal catpipe aside and burst into tears.

CLARA: Poor thing! It was cruel, *wasn't* it, Papa?

SUSY: Well but he oughtn't to done so, in the first place. Cattaraugus wasn't to blame.

CLARA: Why, *Susy!* If Catiline didn't *know* he wasn't allowed—

SUSY: Catiline did know it—Cattaraugus told him so; and besides, Catiline—

CLARA: Cattaraugus only told Catiline that if—

SUSY: Why, *Clara!* Catiline didn't *need* for Cattaraugus to say one single—

Oh, hold on! It's all a mistake! Come to look in the dictionary, we are proceeding from false premises. The Unabridged says a catpipe is "a squeaking instrument used in play-houses to condemn plays." So you see it wasn't a pipe to smoke, after all; Catiline *couldn't* smoke it; therefore it follows that he was simply pretending to smoke it, to stir up his brother, that's all.

SUSY: But, Papa, Catiline might as well smoke as stir up his brother.

CLARA: Susy, you don't like Catiline, and so whatever he does, it don't suit you, it ain't right; and he is only a little fellow, anyway.

SUSY: I don't *approve* of Catiline, but I *like* him well enough; I only say—

CLARA: What is approve?

SUSY: Why it's as if you did something, and I said it was all right. So *I* think he might as well smoke as stir up his brother. Isn't it so, Papa?

Looked at from a strictly mathematical point of view, I don't know, but it *is* a case of six-in-one-and-half-a-dozen-in-the-other. Still, *our* business is mainly with the historical facts; if we only get *them* right, we can leave posterity to take care of the moral aspects of the matter. To resume the thread of the narrative, when Cattaraugus saw that Catiline had not been smoking at all, but had only been making believe, and this too with the avowed object of fraternal aggravation, he was deeply hurt; and by his heat was beguiled into recourse to that bitter weapon, sarcasm; saying, "The Roman Catiline would have betrayed his foe; it was left to the Catasauquian to refine upon the model and betray his friend."

"Oh, a gaudy speech!—and very erudite and swell!" retorted Catiline, derisively, "but just a *little* catachrestic."

SUSY: What is catachrestic, Papa?

"Farfetched," the dictionary says. The remark stung Cattaraugus to the quick, and he called Catiline a catapult; this infuriated Catiline beyond endurance, and he threw down the gauntlet and called Cattaraugus a catso. No cat will stand that; so at it they went. They spat and clawed and fought until they dimmed away and finally disappeared in a flying fog of cat fur.

CLARA: What is a catso, Papa?

"A base fellow, a rogue, a cheat," says the dictionary. When the weather cleared, Cattaraugus, ever ready to acknowledge a fault, whether committed by himself or another, said, "I was wrong, brother—forgive me. A cat may err—to err is cattish; but toward even a foreigner, even a wildcat, a catacaustic remark is in ill taste; how much more so, then, when a brother is the target! Yes, Catiline, I was wrong; I deeply regret the circumstance. Here is my hand—let us forget the dark o'erclouded past in the bright welkin of the present, consecrating ourselves anew to its nobler lessons, and sacrificing ourselves yet again, and forever if need be, to the thrice-armed beacon that binds them in one!"

SUSY: He was a splendid talker, *wasn't* he, Papa? Papa, what is catacaustic?

Well, a catacaustic remark is a bitter, malicious remark—a sort of a—sort of—or a kind of a—well, let's look in the dictionary; that is cheaper. Oh, yes, here it is: "CATACAUSTIC, *n;* a caustic curve formed by reflection of light." Oh, yes, that's it.

SUSY: Well, Papa, what does *that* mean?

SOURCES AND ATTRIBUTIONS

Alligators — *Life on the Mississippi*, 1883

The Ant — *A Tramp Abroad*, 1880

The Ass — *Pudd'nhead Wilson*, 1894

The Australian Magpie — *Following the Equator*, 1897

The Bear on the Boat — *Life on the Mississippi*

Bermuda Spiders — "Notes of an Idle Excursion" in *Tom Sawyer Abroad & Other Stories*, 1896

Bicycle Dogs — "Taming the Bicycle" in *What Is Man? & Other Essays*, 1917

The Boar on the Mountain — *A Tramp Abroad*

Camels — *The Innocents Abroad*, 1869

Camels — *Roughing It*, 1872

The Celebrated Jumping Frog of Calaveras County — *The Celebrated Jumping Frog of Calaveras County and Other Sketches*, 1867

The Chameleon — *Following the Equator*

The Cobra — *Following the Equator*

The Coyote — *Roughing It*

The Dachshund — *Following the Equator*

Delhi Monkeys — *Following the Equator*

The Dingo — *Following the Equator*

The Earl and the Anaconda — *Letters from the Earth*, Edited by Bernard Devoto, 1962

Elephants of Lahore — *Following the Equator*

Eve Figures out How Milk Gets into the Cow — "Eve's Autobiography" in *Letters from the Earth*

A Fable — *The Mysterious Stranger and Other Tales*, 1922

Florentine Flies — *Mark Twain's Autobiography*, 1924

The Genuine Mexican Plug — *Roughing It*

Great Grandfather the Gorilla — *Mark Twain's Letters*, Arranged with comment by Albert Bigelow Paine, 1917

The Hoot Owl — *Mark Twain's Notebook*, Edited by Albert Bigelow Paine, 1935

The Hound Pup — *Roughing It*

Hunting the Deceitful Turkey — *The Mysterious Stranger and Other Tales*

The Indian Crow — *Following the Equator*

Indian Elephants — *Following the Equator*

The Iron Dog — *Roughing It*

The Jackass Rabbit — *Roughing It*

Jericho — *The Innocents Abroad*

Jim Baker's Bluejays — *A Tramp Abroad*

Jim Wolf and the Wasps — *Mark Twain in Eruption*, Edited by Bernard DeVoto, 1940

Joan of Arc's Dragon — *Personal Recollections of Joan of Arc*, 1896